Amyas just wants to be free — free to make his own decisions, not to be forced to marry a human or to have a soul. He's an undine, though, and neither his parents nor his tribe leader listen to him.

Mordred has one goal in life — to make things difficult for the conclave. He left them two hundred years ago, and in that time, he's helped as many supernatural beings as possible. It's not enough to make up for all the ones he killed, though.

When a rogue hero is captured after trying to help the tribe, Amyas knows he has a choice. He can sit back and let everyone else make decisions just like always, or he can take this chance to change his life. It means he'll have to trust the hero, which isn't easy.

But nothing worth having is easy, and this is Amyas's chance to finally take his life into his own hands and live it like he wants. He never expected it would include a hero or that he would fall in love with Mordred. The conclave is hunting the rogue heroes, though, and Amyas's tribe wants him back.

Will he be able to hold on to the happiness he so desperately yearned for? Or will he lose everything, including his first love?

Like Freedom
Copyright © 2021 Catherine Lievens
ISBN: 978-1-4874-3215-7
Cover art by Angela Waters

Published by eXtasy Books Inc or
Devine Destinies, an imprint of eXtasy Books Inc

Look for us online at:
www.eXtasybooks.com or www.devinedestinies.com

Like Freedom
Vikings 4

By

Catherine Lievens

CHAPTER ONE

M ordred was almost ready to leave and go home when his phone vibrated on his desk. He paused in the act of getting to his feet and glared at it. He knew better than not to pick up, so with a sigh, he reached for it. It could mean saving someone, and he wasn't willing to compromise on that.

Sure enough, the text was from one of his people in the heroes who worked for the conclave. Apparently, the conclave was targeting a group of chimeras, and the chimeras would need help. That meant Mordred had to organize a few of his heroes to help them.

He went to work immediately. When possible, he tried to move the targets before the conclave got to them so that everyone could stay out of sight, but it wasn't always possible. Sometimes, the targets wouldn't agree to leave their home, and it was a tricky balance. The conclave already knew about Mordred and his rebels, so they wouldn't be surprised to encounter them, but it would be better for everyone if they managed to stay away from the conclave heroes. The less blood spilled, the better it would be.

He quickly wrote down the details he'd received in the text, deleted it, and used his cell phone to call one of his seconds.

She answered right away, luckily. "I was going to head home," she lamented.

Mordred grinned. "That's fine. I can call Bayard."

Eudocia sighed. "Don't bother him. What's going on?"

Both Eudocia and Bayard worked closely with Mordred. Mordred missed the times when was the one going on missions, but now it was too dangerous. He had a target on his back, and the conclave wouldn't hesitate to shoot if they saw him. That meant that Eudocia and Bayard were the ones who usually went on missions, along with other heroes who worked with them.

"I got news that the conclave is targeting a group of chimeras," Mordred explained.

"Where and when? Do we have time to go there and try to convince them to move?"

"In a few hours, so I'm not sure. I'll email you all the details I have. I'll also keep an eye on the mission from here. You know the drill."

Mordred could hear the humor in Eudocia's voice when she answered. "Take only the people I need, be careful when we get there, try to convince the targets to move, and if we can't, defend them the best we can. I know. It's not my first time."

"I'm very much aware of that," Mordred answered.

He couldn't help that he was worried. He knew what the conclave could do. He'd been a hero for hundreds of years before he'd finally realized something was wrong with what the conclave made them do. He still regretted the things he'd done, but since he'd left, he was working hard to atone for those sins. He liked to think he had, but some days, he realized that nothing could ever atone for that. He'd killed too many innocents, and no matter how many of them he saved, he would never be pardoned for that.

"We'll be fine," Eudocia murmured.

"I hope you will. I need all of you."

It was hell not to be able to go with them. Mordred had done so for many years, so he wasn't rusty. He also made sure to train every day. It wasn't enough, though, not when the conclave was gunning for him. They were especially pissed that Haven had managed to get away from them, even though

Mordred had nothing to do with that. They didn't care, and they wouldn't hesitate to make Mordred pay for that, too. Mordred had every intention to continue doing what he was doing for a long time, which was why he had to be extremely careful these days.

One day, he and the others would defeat the conclave. Most heroes would realize that what they were doing was wrong, and they would turn their back on those people. Until that day came, though, there wasn't much Mordred could do.

"I'll call you when it's done," Eudocia said.

"Make sure you do. And keep the communication open. I need to know if something goes wrong."

He would be following the mission from his office. He always did, even though the people he sent out were more than capable of working on their own. They were all heroes, and the fact that they didn't work for the conclave anymore didn't change that. They knew what they were doing.

They didn't need Mordred. He was the one who had created their secret group, who recruited heroes and had people infiltrating the conclave, but even if he were to die, Eudocia and Bayard would be more than capable of taking his place.

Mordred wouldn't allow that to happen anytime soon, though. He was immortal, and unless he was killed in a very specific way, he would continue living forever. That was more than enough time to push the conclave to their knees and make sure they didn't hurt anyone else.

His cell phone rang as soon as he hung up with Eudocia. He frowned, wondering if it was her, but it wasn't. He recognized the number, and he smiled as he answered. "Haven. I wasn't sure what to think of your silence."

There was a pause before Haven answered. "I wasn't sure whether or not I should call."

"Yet you decided to. How come?"

"I wanted to talk about your offer."

Mordred couldn't help but smile. He was always happy to recruit a hero, but Haven especially so, because he came with Dimitri. Dimitri was a leshy, and while Mordred's little group was mostly made up of heroes, he would be a good fit if he decided to fight with them. It would help Mordred's rebels to see they truly could work with supernatural creatures instead of killing them.

That depended on what Haven and Dimitri would do, though. "What did you want to talk about?" he asked.

"How does it work?"

"It's not hard. I'm the head of our group. I have several people infiltrated in the conclave, which means that I usually manage to get information about who they're targeting and when they plan to do it."

"The conclave has to know that."

"I have no doubt they do. They have no idea who's spying for me, though, and things will stay that way. When I lose one of my informers, I have more in place, and I'm recruiting more all the time." There was also the fact that he had an informer in the conclave itself, but that was one of his most important secrets, and he wasn't about to tell anyone, let alone someone he barely knew.

"So you get information before the conclave sends someone," Haven said.

"I do, and I use that knowledge to send a team of my heroes to help whoever is being targeted. Right now, it's a group of chimeras."

"What do you do?"

"Usually, try to move them. It works most of the time, but not always. Some creatures don't want to leave the homes they built, and I understand that, even though it would be safer. When that happens, we try to convince the heroes who arrive from the Conclave to change their mind about who they're working for, and if that doesn't work, well, you can imagine."

The heroes who couldn't see how wrong the conclave was usually ended up dead. They were mostly sent out alone or with one other hero, while Mordred and his people only moved in groups. That meant the conclave heroes were usually numerically inferior, and the people fighting them knew exactly how to kill them.

Mordred didn't enjoy doing it, but it was necessary.

"You're the one who decides who gets to be saved," Haven continued.

"Everyone deserves to be saved. If I get word that the conclave targets someone, I send my people, whoever and whatever they are. I can repeat that time and time again, but you don't have to believe me. Why don't you come to our headquarters? You can spend some time here, see how we work, and make your decision."

"What about Dimitri?"

"He's welcome, just like you are. Bring him with you. If he wants, he can even work with us."

"You would let a supernatural creature work with you?"

"It's what we all are, in the end. We might be heroes, but we're not human anymore." That was the one thing the conclave refused to admit, because if they did, they'd also have to admit they were killing supernatural creatures for power and not because they were a danger to humanity.

They would never do that, but it wouldn't stop Mordred from doing what was right.

"You should do what your sister did," Amyas's mom said.

It took a lot of work for Amyas not to sigh. "I don't want to marry a human," he said through gritted teeth.

"Of course you do."

"You didn't marry a human, yet you're fine."

Amyas's mom looked like she wanted to yell at him. He was lucky she didn't, because he didn't like it when people yelled. "I married your father because I couldn't find a human to marry. You know what it means for us."

Amyas *did* sigh this time. "I don't want a soul."

His mother looked scandalized. "Everyone wants a soul. It's why we marry humans. Just look at your sister. She's perfectly happy."

"And she'll die in a few decades. Why would I want that?"

Amyas's mother shook her head. "Why wouldn't you? You have to want a soul. We all do."

Amyas really didn't. He understood his parents wanted him to find a human and marry her so he could get his own soul, but he didn't want to lose his immortality, even though he wasn't doing much with it.

He and his family lived in a lake, like most undines. They were water creatures, after all. That meant that if they wanted to find a human husband or wife, they had to leave their home and go to a human city or town, which was what Amyas's sister had done. Now she would never be able to live in the lake again. She had to stay with her husband and make sure he didn't cheat on her. If he did, well, things wouldn't go well for either of them. That was one thing Amyas's mother was avoiding talking about. If she pushed, though, he wouldn't hesitate to bring it up.

His sister wasn't immortal anymore, and while they'd never been close, he could only imagine what it was like to be mortal. He didn't think it was worth a soul to lose immortality, even though every undine wanted exactly that.

Amyas had never wanted it. He didn't want to lose his immortality, but he also didn't want to depend on whatever human he ended up marrying. If that human cheated, the human would die, while Amyas would be immortal again. He wasn't like his sister, who could get pregnant and have a baby. If she managed to make that happen before her husband cheated on her, she would stay human while he would die.

Amyas was pretty sure his sister didn't care much about her husband. She wanted to be mortal and to have a soul, and she did. As soon as she got pregnant and had the baby, her husband wouldn't matter anymore. If he cheated, she would be able to find someone else, maybe someone she truly loved instead of someone she'd managed to convince to marry her.

There was too much unknown in that kind of situation for Amyas to want to be part of anything like it. He liked being immortal, and he didn't think that having a soul made you that different from someone who didn't have one. He didn't see the need for one, but his parents wouldn't listen to him.

They never would. They'd wanted to find a human to marry when they were younger, but they hadn't, and they'd ended up marrying each other. They still complained about that, even though they loved each other.

Well, Amyas hoped they did.

They'd never been warm parents, and Amyas and his sister had learned not to ask too much of them. They were over the moon that Amyas's sister had found a human, and now they were pushing for him to do the same. They would never stop pushing, and the only respite he had was when he left the house.

"I'm going to go," he said.

His mother frowned. "We're talking."

"We were, but I don't see a reason for us to continue. You won't change my mind, and I won't change yours."

"We're undines. Finding a human husband or wife is crucial to us."

"To you, maybe. It doesn't mean all of us want the same thing." Amyas knew his mother wouldn't accept anything he said.

It wasn't respectful to leave in the middle of a conversation, but he did anyway, ignoring his mother calling for him to come back. He was done talking about this. He wasn't his sister, and he didn't care about finding a human to marry, which meant he wouldn't. He supposed he should feel lucky that now he could marry a male, but that didn't change anything. Amyas preferred males, but he still didn't want to marry anyone.

He left the house and swam away from the village. He needed peace, but he wouldn't get any if he stayed home. Anyone he saw would want to talk to him and congratulate him on his sister's wedding, which he couldn't care less about.

He swam toward the waterfall, knowing he would have some peace there. Maybe he could even sing. As long as he was alone and no one annoyed him, he didn't care what he did.

He smiled when his head breached the surface of the water. He pushed his long hair behind his back, where it stuck to his skin, and climbed the rocks under the waterfall. From there, he could watch the forest around the lake without anyone noticing him, which was something he did often.

Most humans stayed away from the lake. They knew about it, but it was deep in the forest, and it would be hard for them to get there. A few managed, though, and Amyas was always fascinated.

But not enough to marry one of them and lose his immortality.

He settled onto one of the rocks, but before he could start singing, he noticed something moving in the forest. He grinned and leaned closer to the sheet of water in front of him, wondering who it might be. It was usually animals, but he didn't mind. He was as fascinated with them as he was with humans.

He frowned when two men stepped closer to the lake. They

were both holding swords, which didn't bode well. Humans didn't usually use swords, not anymore. It was an ancient weapon.

Heroes used swords, and Amyas held his breath as he watched them poke around.

Why were they here? There was only one answer to that question, and it was that they were trying to find the undines. Amyas didn't know how they'd found out undines lived in the lake, although he supposed it was a fair bet, considering the lake was isolated and deep.

He stayed as still as he could as they continued looking around. He didn't want them to notice him. They wouldn't hesitate to kill him, because that was what heroes did. They killed supernatural creatures, because they thought they didn't deserve to live.

Amyas tightened his hands into fists, but he didn't move. He had to let the tribe know what was happening. They had to be careful when they left the lake — if heroes were poking their noses around, it meant they knew undines lived here and that they were trying to get their hands on them.

CHAPTER TWO

M ordred grinned when the portal opened in front of him. He always felt giddy when he welcomed new members to his rebel team. They needed more people, and Haven and Dimitri would be perfect. Mordred would have to convince them this was the right thing to do first, but he was positive he could, especially after talking to Haven on the phone.

"Welcome," he said as they stepped through.

Haven looked wary, but Dimitri was smiling. "Thank you," he said. He looked around. "I have to say that this isn't what I expected."

"Let me guess—you thought you were going to find us in a warehouse or something like that."

"I did. I'm pleased to see that's not the case."

"I chose this place because I wanted the heroes who work with me to be able to enjoy life outside of the job," Mordred said as he gestured at the house behind him—well, the mansion.

The house was his. He'd lived hundreds of years, and he'd managed to accumulate a lot of money. He hadn't needed it when he was a hero for the conclave, but as soon as he'd left, he'd used the money to buy a massive house in the middle of the forest, and of course, he was the one financing the entire operation. A few heroes insisted on helping, and Mordred never said no, because they needed to feel like this was a group effort, but he could continue paying for hundreds of years, and he would still be rich.

"So the heroes live here?" Dimitri asked.

"Not all of them. Some would rather have their own place, and while it can be dangerous, I never say no. After the life they lived, they deserve their privacy. Besides, they're only one portal away."

"The conclave doesn't follow your portals?" Haven intervened.

"Just like you, we use portals the conclave can't find. They also can't find this place. I've worked with witches and mages, and they made sure that only the people I want to be able to find the house do so."

"It's impressive," Haven said grudgingly.

Mordred's smile widened. "I'm glad you feel that way. If you decide to work with us, you won't have to live here, but you're welcome to."

"Isn't it crowded? How many heroes work for you?"

This was delicate information, and Mordred wouldn't give it just to anyone. Haven wasn't anyone, though. He'd left the conclave, and he was with Dimitri. He knew how wrong the conclave was to kill supernatural creatures just because of what they were, and Mordred trusted him. He might regret it, but he didn't think that would be the case. He and Thor had talked, and Thor trusted Haven. That meant Mordred did, too.

"It can be crowded," he admitted. "But there's more than enough space for everyone to have their own set of rooms. By that, I mean that each hero has a bedroom, a private bathroom, and a sitting room in which they can entertain people. Everyone uses the kitchen, living room, and other communal spaces. There's a library, too."

Dimitri's eyes glittered. "A library?"

"And everyone is welcome to anything in it, of course. Why don't I give you a tour?"

Haven grumbled, but Dimitri seemed more than eager to follow Mordred.

Mordred stepped under an arch and crossed over to the front door, which he threw open. "Welcome." He knew what Haven and Dimitri were seeing, and he hoped they liked it.

The entrance looked like it belonged in a castle. The walls and floors were made of polished stone, and a chandelier hung from the ceiling. Most of the house was built in stone and wood, which Mordred loved.

He guided Haven and Dimitri through the house toward the kitchen. "This is where the magic happens," he joked as they stepped in. The wide windows let in a lot of light. "It's one of my favorite rooms," he admitted.

"Who cooks?" Haven asked.

"Whoever wants to cook. A lot of the time, a few of us cook for everyone. It's not something we expect, though, so if you're hungry, just open the fridge and grab something. You're also welcome to keep food in your rooms."

"This is pretty," Dimitri commented.

"Thank you."

"I especially like the contrast between wood and stone. This *really* isn't what I expected."

Mordred wasn't surprised. When people found out what he did, they expected him to guide the rebel heroes like an army, while they were more like a family. Not all of them were close, which was why only some of the heroes who worked with Mordred lived in the house. Eudocia and Bayard were two of those heroes.

Mordred continued walking through the house, showing Haven and Dimitri where they could live if they wanted to. "As you can see, the table has places for everyone to sit around it, and the living room is wide enough."

"Is that an inside balcony?" Dimitri asked, his gaze upward.

Mordred couldn't stop smiling. He felt like a child, showing his home. "It is. From there, you can see from upstairs."

"It's gorgeous," Dimitri murmured.

Both he and Haven looked a bit dazed by the time they finished walking through the ground floor. Mordred had shown them the library, his office, and every other room they might be interested in. "I won't show you the bedrooms. I'm sure you understand they're private."

"Of course," Dimitri said.

"There's also an elevator, but we don't use it often. It will be handy if you have to move a lot of things." Mordred paused. "That is, if you decide to move here. Even if you agree to work with us, you don't actually have to."

"We'll have to talk about it," Dimitri said.

"I didn't expect anything different. I'd like an answer right away, as I'm sure you can understand, but I won't push for one."

"You only work with heroes?" Haven asked.

"As you know, I don't. I often work with Thor, and sometimes with his friends. No supernatural creature lives here with us, though."

"Dimitri would be the only one?"

"He would, but he would be welcome. No one would try to push him away or tell him he doesn't belong."

"You can't be sure of that."

"I can be. I don't control every single hero, even though they work with me. All of them are here for a reason. They realized that what the conclave is doing to supernatural creatures isn't right. They want that to change, and all of them have been on several missions to save different kinds of creatures. You don't trust them, but I do. I hope it's going to be enough for the two of you to give us a chance."

Mordred wanted to say more, but his phone beeped in his pocket. He briefly closed his eyes. He'd hoped to have some time away from work, but he should have known better. "If you'll excuse me?" he asked.

Haven nodded curtly and turned his attention to Dimitri, so Mordred stepped away and took his phone out. He frowned at the text on the screen.

C sent two heroes to poke around an undine village.

It was followed by coordinates, no doubt to the village. Mordred knew better than to answer. He quickly copied and pasted the coordinates, then deleted the text. When he turned his attention to Haven and Dimitri again, they were both staring.

"Work?" Dimitri asked.

Mordred nodded. "The conclave is poking around where they shouldn't be. I have to send a team." The problem was that most of them were already out. He could call Eudocia or Bayard and check with them whether anyone was available, but Haven and Dimitri were with him, which was kind of perfect. "Actually, *we* could be that team."

Dimitri blinked, while Haven's expression hardened. "You want to put Dimitri in danger before he even agrees to work with you?"

Dimitri slapped Haven's chest. "Stop acting like a caveman. I'm here, and I can say yes or no." He looked at Mordred. "And in this case, I agree. I want to come."

"You're not a hero," Haven said.

Dimitri glared at him. "I know you're trying to protect me, and I'm grateful, but don't offend me. I might not be a hero, but that doesn't mean I can't defend myself. You should know."

Haven stared at him for a moment before nodding. "All right. Stay close to me, though."

Dimitri rolled his eyes but nodded. "Of course."

Mordred was elated. This was the perfect way to show both Dimitri and Haven they should be working with Mordred and his people. They'd be able to see what Mordred did, and hopefully, they would agree it was necessary and that Mordred's organization needed them.

The heroes were back. Amyas didn't know what to think, but he knew what they'd come for, and he dreaded it.

This time, he'd arrived at the waterfall before the heroes appeared. Since he was already there, he stayed as quiet and still as he could and watched them. He knew Necsa would be aware of the heroes' presence. He'd warned her the first time he'd seen them, so she knew to keep an eye out. She would no doubt send someone to fight the heroes and send them away, and Amyas wanted to see it.

He'd always been more interested in what happened outside the village than inside it. He knew everyone in the village, knew their parents and their children — and their secrets. He was ready for something different.

He only had to wait a few minutes before undine warriors started coming out of the lake. One of the heroes noticed and took a step back, his expression morphing to worry. Amyas would be worried, too, if he was faced with *that*.

Undines were usually peaceful, and the heroes were clearly surprised at seeing that wouldn't be the case this time. Necsa and the village had learned to defend themselves. With the conclave hunting supernatural creatures left and right, they'd needed to. Now, the village had several groups of warriors who stepped in when their leader told them to, which she had. Amyas wouldn't have the faintest idea where to start, but then, everyone in the village expected him to leave once he found a human spouse, so it wouldn't be useful for him to learn.

The hero who had noticed the warriors elbowed the other. They stared and quickly talked to each other, and Amyas waited to see what would happen. That was the only reason he noticed the portal opening. The undine warriors were focused on the two conclave heroes, so they didn't see the other two coming out of a portal that had appeared between the trees.

Amyas's eyes widened when he saw those two heroes weren't alone.

Heroes didn't like supernatural beings, so why was a leshy accompanying these two? They were also dressed differently than the first two heroes. None of it made sense, and Amyas had no idea what was happening. Were they there to help the other heroes or to fight them? He wouldn't have thought that possible, because all heroes were bad people, but these were with a leshy. The woodland creature wouldn't be with them if they were dangerous to him.

Amyas wanted answers, which was the only reason he stayed where he was and watched what was happening. He knew what Necsa would think. Most of the village would agree with her that all heroes were bad, no matter what. Amyas wasn't so sure about that, though. Just like undines, heroes had their own personalities and thoughts. Maybe the two new heroes didn't work for the conclave. Amyas had never heard of such a thing, but there could be a first time for everything, including this. It was the only explanation he could think of for what was happening in front of him.

The strange heroes moved toward the first two, and when those tried to open a portal to leave, the new heroes stopped them. One of them tried talking to them, but the heroes didn't seem to want to listen to him.

Amyas would have. Heroes could be very different from one another. The only thing they shared was the birthmark that identified them as heroes. The one talking was tall and had dark hair. Amyas could see something glinting on his ears, but he was fascinated by the hero's hands that moved in front of him as he urgently spoke.

The problem was that the first two heroes had no intention of listening. They both drew their swords, and the fight began.

Mordred's experience was the only reason he didn't freak out at the sight in front of him. Were those people standing in the water undine warriors? That didn't make sense. Undines were peaceful water elemental beings. Their main objective in life was to find a human to marry and possibly have children with them. Mordred had never heard of any of them fighting, but he couldn't deny what was in front of him, and he wished he'd noticed sooner. He wouldn't have tried talking to the heroes if he had.

The undine warriors were fast, and they managed to surround both the two heroes Mordred had been trying to stop and Mordred, Haven, and Dimitri. They didn't seem to care that Dimitri was obviously a supernatural being. They looked fierce, and like they were about to kick ass.

Which they did before Mordred could try to explain what he and his friends were doing there.

They attacked, and Mordred had no more time to marvel at the fact that they were fighting. He had to defend himself, which was harder than expected. Since he knew undines weren't usually warriors, he hadn't expected them to be able to fight, but he'd been wrong. They *could* fight, and they were pretty good at it, too.

Mordred took it as an opportunity to watch Haven and Dimitri. Just like Dimitri had said, he knew what he was doing, even though he was obviously less experienced than Haven. He held his own, though, using the plants and trees around him, at least until three warriors surrounded him. Then Haven stepped in, and Dimitri didn't protest when Haven slammed one of the warriors against a tree. He punched a second one right in the face, and Dimitri took the opportunity to kick the last one between the legs.

Something heavy landed against Mordred's side, and he had to focus on his own fight. They were losing, though. He'd hoped they would be able to overthrow the undines, but the warriors were too good, which meant they had to run. Mordred didn't like it, but he would, if it meant protecting Haven and Dimitri.

Someone pushed him against a tree and punched the breath out of his lungs. He managed to turn before the undine could hurt him, ducking and nailing the undine with a fist in the side. The undine responded by raising his sword and hitting Mordred on the side of the head. Mordred's ears rang, and he saw double for a moment. It was enough for the undine to hit him again. Mordred slid to his knees, feeling like he was about to throw up.

He noticed Dimitri moving toward him, but he shook his head and raised a hand. "Create a portal," he yelled. "Go back to the house. My seconds will know what to do."

The undine hit Mordred a third time. The last thing he saw was Dimitri and Haven running through the portal.

When he opened his eyes, he briefly wondered if he was dead. A group of blonde people with blue eyes stood around him, staring at him. He knew better than to think they were angels, though. Undines were all blonde with blue eyes, at least the full-blooded ones.

Mordred blinked. His head hurt as if someone had hit it several times, which, if he remembered right, had actually happened. His blood pulsed in his brain, and he blinked again, hoping that the fact that he still couldn't see right would fix itself.

He looked around. He wasn't the only one who'd been captured. One of the two heroes he'd been trying to stop was there, too. They were both tied to a pole on the shore. There were other poles, but they were empty, which helped

Mordred relax. Dimitri and Haven had managed to get away, which meant that someone would eventually come for Mordred.

"Good. You're awake."

Mordred turned to look at the woman who had spoken. She was tall, with blonde hair falling around her face. Her blue eyes were hard, and he knew he was standing in front of someone in charge.

"I wouldn't have been unconscious if someone hadn't hit me repeatedly on the head," Mordred pointed out.

The woman arched a brow. "You're a funny one, aren't you?"

"I do my best."

"It won't help you in this situation."

"I didn't think it would. I can't change who I am, though." And wasting time meant he was able to take in more details of what was happening around him.

She stared at him for a moment. "Does that include being a hero?"

Mordred swallowed. He eyed the hero next to him. He didn't want to tell this woman who he was, not when the hero might go back to the conclave and tell them everything he'd learned.

"He won't help you," the woman said.

"I wasn't looking for help. I'm a hero, yes. I can't change that, because it's what I was born as, just like you were born an undine. It doesn't mean I work for the conclave, though."

The woman's eyes narrowed. "Your name?"

Mordred swallowed. "Mordred. I haven't worked for the conclave in two hundred years."

She nodded curtly. "I see. It doesn't matter. Once a hero, always a hero."

"And you are? Because I introduced myself, but you haven't."

"Necsa. I'm the leader of this village."

Mordred had already guessed that, but he didn't say it out loud. He felt like Necsa wouldn't appreciate it if he did. "It's a pleasure to meet you."

She softly snorted. "I doubt it is. Tell me, why shouldn't I kill you right away?"

"Because I'm not here to hurt your village. I'm here to save it."

"As you saw, we're more than able to save ourselves."

Mordred couldn't deny she was right. "I didn't know about that. I heard the conclave was poking around trying to find your village, and I wanted to help. I don't work for the conclave." Mordred doubted Necsa would change her mind about him, no matter how many times he said it.

"How can I be sure you're not lying?"

"You can't be, not a hundred percent. You're going to have to give me the benefit of the doubt."

She stepped back, and Mordred knew she wouldn't. He'd expected it, but he was still disappointed. He hoped he could get out of the situation on his own. He didn't want his people to fight with Necsa and her warriors. The heroes would win, but at what cost?

"I won't take a chance on a hero. It doesn't matter who you work for. You and your people have been killing people like me for hundreds of years." She turned toward the lake.

"You saw me with a leshy," Mordred tried. It was his last chance to make her rethink this.

She paused just long enough to say, "Unfortunately, some supernatural beings are ready to do anything to survive, even give up on their people and fraternize with the enemy."

With that, she stepped into the lake. Her warriors went after her, leaving Mordred and the hero tied to the poles. They were alone, but Mordred had no doubt that someone was watching them. He could feel it, and no matter how anxious it made him, he knew he needed to ignore it. If he wanted to make it out of the situation, he would have to find his way out. He couldn't wait for his people to come, because it would cost too many lives for them to fight the undines.

That might be his only chance to make it out of this alive, though.

Amyas didn't know what to do. He wanted to stay at the surface and watch the two heroes, see what the strange one did, but he knew Necsa wanted to talk to the village. He should be there. If he wasn't, someone would notice, and he had no doubt his parents or Necsa herself would have something to say about that.

He slipped off the rocks and into the water, then quickly swam to the village. Everyone was gathered at the entrance, where Necsa stood on a rock, looking at the tribe. Amyas managed to wiggle his way between people until he was right under her.

"We won," Necsa declared.

The crowd around Amyas screamed and cheered. He couldn't bring himself to do that, though. He knew something was wrong, but he wasn't sure Necsa or anyone else would listen to him if he told them. He knew better than to interrupt Necsa right now, so he pressed his lips together and listened to what she was saying.

She raised her hands, and the crowd quieted. She nodded, obviously satisfied. "We defeated the heroes and the conclave. They'll pay for what they did."

"They didn't do anything," Amyas pointed out. He couldn't keep quiet. He was pretty sure at least a few people turned to glare at him, but he kept his gaze on Necsa.

She stared back. "How would you know that?"

"I was at the surface when they arrived. I wanted to come

back, but I was afraid they would notice me, so I stayed still. I saw everything."

"Then you saw we fought and that we won."

"I did. But the strange hero didn't come with the other two. He was there to fight them, not to do whatever they were doing."

Necsa snorted. "Did you hear the conversation I had with him?"

Amyas hadn't. The waterfall was too noisy, and he'd been too far. "No."

"Then you don't know anything about the situation. Once a hero, always a hero. He'll die right along with the other."

Amyas's heart felt like it sank to the bottom of his stomach. "You're going to kill them?"

"I will." Necsa narrowed her eyes. "And you and I will have a conversation about you being out of the lake when it happened. You should know better."

"I wasn't doing anything. Since when aren't we allowed to leave the lake?" It didn't make sense. How were undines supposed to meet humans if they couldn't leave the lake?

Necsa looked around again. "I know everyone here wants to find a human to marry. I understand. Being out of the lake right now is dangerous, though. Heroes know we're here, which means the conclave does, too. All of you need to be careful and stay in the village for now." She turned her attention to Amyas again. "That includes you."

"But—"

Necsa glared at Amyas, and he snapped his mouth shut. A hand squeezed his shoulder. He turned to see his father standing beside him, looking worried. Amyas pressed his lips together. If he wanted to talk to Necsa and try to convince her to let the strange hero go, he needed to do it when she was alone. She wouldn't want to listen to him when the entire village was there.

Now that Necsa was done talking, the crowd dispersed. Amyas's father guided him toward their house, and Amyas allowed him to do so. His mother was there, too, and as soon as the front door was close behind them, they both turned to face him.

"What were you thinking?" his mother asked.

Amyas crossed his arms over his chest and glared. "I was thinking that it wouldn't be fair to kill someone who was here to protect us rather than hurt us."

"You heard what Necsa said. The heroes want to hurt us. She's our leader for a reason. She knows better than you."

Amyas hesitated. They weren't wrong, at least when it came to defending the village. Amyas thought Necsa had been doing a good job since she'd been chosen, but she wasn't perfect. "You didn't see what I saw. The strange hero was here to help us. I'm sure of that."

"Necsa will make the decision. She's our leader. You're not," Amyas's father said. "You need to forget this. It won't do you or our family any good if you keep pushing. Necsa listened to you, and she answered your questions."

"She won't listen to reason. How can she know what the strange hero wants if she doesn't talk to him again?"

"She already talked to him. She got the answers she wanted and expected. Stay out of this, Amyas. She's been lenient with you for now, but she won't be for much longer if you continue pushing her like this."

"I want her to do the right thing. How is that pushing?"

Amyas's mother grabbed his wrist and squeezed. It hurt, and he tried to snatch it back, but she didn't let it go. "Listen to your father," she said curtly. "We both want the best for you, and so does Necsa. This isn't your business, and you have to stay out of it. You need to focus on finding a wife."

Amyas glared. "I already told you I don't want to get married, least of all to a human."

"And we already told you it's your duty. We want what's best for our children, and that's a soul."

Amyas pulled again, and this time, his mother let him go. "If you want what's best for me, shouldn't *I* be the one to decide what that is? I'm an adult. I know what I want and what I'm doing, and just like this situation isn't my business, my life isn't yours."

"It is while you live under our roof," Amyas's father said.

Amyas was used to this kind of answer from his parents. "I still live here only because there are no homes available in the village."

"You'll find yourself a human wife and move in with her eventually. Now go to your room."

Amyas glared and shook his head. "I might still live with you, but I don't have to obey you. If you have something against it, I'm sure I can find a rock to sleep on." Amyas turned around and headed toward the door.

He slammed it shut behind himself, grinning in pleasure at the sound it made and at his parents calling for him behind it. He didn't give them time to open the door. He didn't want to talk to them right now, and he didn't want to have to face them. He wanted to think about the strange hero and why he was here, so that was what he would do.

Necsa had told him to stay in the water, but that didn't mean he had to stay in the village. He swam out, headed toward the waterfall. He didn't swim to the surface again. Instead, he stayed under the water. He enjoyed feeling the force of the waterfall push down on his shoulders. He sat on a rock, crossed his legs, and thought.

The strange hero and his two friends had been there to help. Amyas was sure of that, even though he didn't think he could convince anyone. Necsa was going to kill an innocent, and Amyas didn't know how to stop her. He had to, though. He would never forgive himself if he didn't do at least something to save the strange hero. But if he did, it would put him in the spotlight, and Necsa wouldn't be happy. If he was lucky, she would banish him. If he wasn't, he would die along with the heroes.

Amyas had a decision to make. His heart raced as he thought about the options, even though he already knew which one he'd choose. He wanted out of the village. He wanted out of this life in which the most important thing he could do was find himself a human to marry. He wanted to explore the world, and he would never have that opportunity if he stayed in the lake.

He might get himself killed if he tried helping the hero, but it was the right thing to do, and Amyas wanted to do it.

CHAPTER THREE

"We wouldn't be here if you hadn't intervened," the hero tied up to the other pole snapped.

Mordred examined him. He'd learned the names of as many heroes as he could, thanks to his sources inside the conclave. He was pretty sure this one was Percival, but he wouldn't swear to it. "And where would you be if I hadn't?"

"Back at the conclave. Because of you, we're both trapped here. You know they're going to try to kill us."

"I expect them to, yes, after what their leader said. It's understandable, considering you and your friend were thinking about killing them." So far, Mordred wasn't too worried. He didn't enjoy being tied to a pole and having to chat with a hero who clearly wasn't ready to hear what he had to say, but he'd been in worse situations, and he trusted his people. They would get here, and they would free him. As for Percival, Mordred wasn't sure.

"I'm a hero. I obey the orders the conclave gives me," Percival snapped. "You wouldn't know about that, though. You're clearly a deserter."

Mordred grinned. "I am. Did the conclave tell you about me?"

"Why should they?"

That was interesting. Mordred had expected the conclave to tell the heroes to be careful when it came to him, maybe to kill him on sight. Instead, they were apparently hiding what Mordred and his people were doing. "What did the conclave tell you to do with rogue heroes?"

"To kill all of you. You've been tainted by those creatures, and you don't do your job anymore. You're not useful."

Mordred tsked. "I resent that. I like to think I'm very useful." Although not to the conclave, he supposed.

Percival tried to pull on the ties keeping him prisoner, but they didn't budge. "I need to get away from here."

"You won't. You'll have to wait, just like I am."

Percival glared. "The conclave won't save you. Whoever they send will focus on me, and we'll leave you here. It'll teach you not to stick your nose in conclave business and to walk the right path."

"And *what* is the right path? To blindly obey every order the conclave gives you? Don't you have your own mind and your own thoughts? Can't you be critical of them and what they ask you to do?" Although Mordred supposed they didn't actually ask. The conclave *ordered*, and they expected to be obeyed. If they weren't, the hero who had gone against them met their fate. It was never a nice one, which was why Mordred had left as soon as he'd realized what the conclave was doing and what they would do to him if they knew he was aware of it.

He leaned his head back against the pole and looked at the sky. He'd spent the entire night tied up, and it was starting to get old. He wished his people would come, but he understood why they wanted to be careful. They didn't know what they would be up against, not when undines were usually peaceful. These clearly weren't, and since they were organized when it came to warriors and defense, Mordred's rescuers would have to be careful. Still, his ass hurt from sitting on the ground for so long, and he was hungry.

He didn't realize he'd closed his eyes until he snapped them open when he heard a voice. He looked around, but he couldn't see anyone. He was sure he could hear someone singing, though. It had to come from the lake, which meant it was an undine.

The voice was incredible. It was smooth and warm, and it helped Mordred relax, which wasn't what he'd intended to do. He was hoping he'd be able to meet whoever was singing when he noticed the water was rippling. A blond head poked through the surface, followed by the rest of the undine's body.

It was a male, and he was gorgeous. Mordred usually had relationships with other heroes. That was much simpler, because they knew what his life was like and they understood his mission. He supposed it was also comfortable. He knew what to expect from another hero, including their body type. All of them were born to fight, and it showed. They were tall and muscled, and they added onto that with training.

The undine was different, though. He was short, almost a foot shorter than Mordred, if Mordred was right about his estimate. He was also thin, and even though his body was wrapped in some strange glistening fabric that looked like it was made from algae, Mordred doubted there were many muscles to see. He didn't care, though. That didn't take away from the undine's beauty.

He was blond, and his eyes were blue. That was the case with most full-blooded undines, but for whatever reason, Mordred found this one even more beautiful than the others he'd seen yesterday.

"What the fuck do you want?" Percival snapped.

Mordred glared at him. "Can't you be nice for one second?"

"He's keeping us prisoner. Why should I be nice?"

"Maybe because he's holding food?"

Percival's eyes narrowed, and he looked at the undine again.

Mordred grinned when Percival's gaze went to the basket the undine was holding. Then he turned his attention to the undine, smiling. "Thank you," he said. He was pretty sure the undines' leader hadn't ordered for food to be brought out. She was going to kill Mordred and Percival, so why would she care if they had food before they died?

The undine hesitated. "I'm sorry you're here," he said. His voice was as beautiful as he was, even when he wasn't singing.

"It's not your fault. You didn't make this decision. My name is Mordred, and this is Percival. What's yours?"

Percival made a strangled sound. "How do you know my name?" he asked.

Mordred ignored him, focusing on the undine instead. The undine hesitated, but the corner of his lips curled into a tiny smile. "I'm Amyas."

"Well, it's a pleasure to meet you, Amyas, although I wish it were under different circumstances."

Amyas nodded and came to crouch next to Mordred. He opened his basket, frowned as he took in the fact that Mordred's hands were tied up, then slid something out of the basket and unwrapped it. He discarded the algae, broke a piece of whatever the food was off, and held it up to Mordred's lips.

Mordred prayed Amyas wasn't trying to poison him and opened his mouth. It was fish, and he chewed before swallowing. He tried to ignore the brush of Amyas's fingers against his lips, because that was *not* the way his thoughts should turn in this situation. "Thank you," he said.

Amyas slowly nodded. "Why are you here?" he asked.

"Didn't Necsa tell you?"

"She said you're here to hurt us. To destroy the village. That's why she wants to kill you."

Amyas looked sorry, and while Mordred shared that feeling, he didn't want Amyas to feel guilty. "She'd already decided to kill us before she went back into the lake."

"She doesn't believe you're not dangerous to us."

Mordred blinked. "Why do you think that?" He was

hoping Amyas might help. He still had faith in his team, but having help from Amyas would make everything easier. If Amyas freed Mordred, Mordred could create a portal and be out of here in seconds. He wasn't sure what he would do with Percival if that happened, but he supposed he didn't have to think about it just yet. He was still tied up, after all.

"I saw you when you arrived. You don't look like the other hero, and I saw you were with a leshy. He wouldn't work with you if you were dangerous to him or to us."

"You're right. I was here to help protect your village. I found out that the conclave had sent someone here, and I wanted to stop them."

"You're a hero, though."

"I'll always be a hero because it's what I was born as. I don't work for the conclave, though. I haven't worked for the conclave in two hundred years. What they're doing is wrong, so instead, I'm working against them, trying to save as many supernatural creatures and people as I can."

A noise coming from the lake made both of them turn toward it. Amyas was tense, and since Mordred suspected he wasn't supposed to be there, he understood. He didn't want Amyas to get caught, either. "You should go," he murmured.

Amyas frowned. "I should give the other hero food."

"I won't eat anything you give me," Percival snapped.

If Mordred had his way, he would have a nice chat with Percival about being rude to people helping them. He might work for the conclave, but that didn't mean he had to be an idiot.

Mordred smiled at Amyas. "You heard him. Finish feeding me. Then you should go. We'll be fine."

Amyas looked like he wanted to say no, but instead, he nodded. He quickly fed Mordred the last of the fish, then, with one last glance behind himself, disappeared into the lake. Mordred watched until the water stilled and it looked like Amyas had never been here.

"I can't believe you ate that food. How do you know it wasn't poisoned?" Percival asked.

Mordred sighed. "You really *are* an idiot, aren't you?"

"You can't talk to me that way."

"I can talk to you any way I want. I know you still believe what the conclave tells you about supernatural creatures, but Amyas was trying to help us. I hope you didn't fuck it up with your attitude."

Mordred didn't know what to think, but he had hope. Amyas had been here to help, and he might do more. That meant Mordred had another chance to make it out of the situation alive.

Amyas rushed back to the village, hiding the basket behind a rock and hoping no one had noticed his absence. He wasn't supposed to have contact with the heroes. No one in the village except for Necsa and her warriors were. Amyas had been curious, though, and he'd wanted to find out what was going on.

He'd been right. Mordred had come to help the village, not to attack it. He doubted Necsa would listen to him if he tried telling her, though. She'd already made her decision to kill Mordred and Percival.

Amyas didn't care much about Percival. He'd been rude, and Amyas didn't like him. That didn't mean he deserved to die, but he *had* come to attack the village, after all. Mordred hadn't, though, and if Amyas could do anything for him, he wanted to.

Where was he supposed to start, though? He couldn't go to Necsa, not if he didn't want to be punished, and the next best thing was talking to his parents. They might be able to talk to Necsa and to make her see how wrong she was. Amyas might be an adult, but he was still young. His parents had known Necsa before she became the leader, and hopefully, it would mean something to her.

He pushed open the front door, going straight to the kitchen when he heard his parents' voices. His mother was preparing food, and Amyas took a moment to watch her and his father. If he were to leave, he would miss them, but that wouldn't be enough to stop him. He wanted freedom. Maybe once Mordred was free and safe, Amyas could leave the lake and never come back. It was tempting, but first, he had something to do.

"I went to talk to the heroes," he declared.

His mother jerked, almost dropping the fish she'd been cleaning. His father turned around, obviously scared. "What are you talking about?" he asked.

"I went to talk to the heroes. I wanted to find out why one of them was different, and I was right. Mordred was here to help us, not to hurt us."

"Mordred?" Amyas's mother asked in a shrill voice.

"The strange hero. He's the one who was dressed differently, and the one who was working with a leshy. I knew something was off, and I was right. He was here to help us fight the heroes who wanted to hurt us. We can't allow Necsa to hurt him."

Amyas's father strode toward him. He grabbed Amyas's shoulders and looked down at him. "You disobeyed Necsa's orders. You went to talk to the heroes even though she told everyone to stay in the village. What were you thinking?"

Amyas pulled away. "That I needed to do the right thing. Do you really want an innocent man to be killed because he was trying to help us?"

"He lied to you. You can't trust anything a hero says. You need to stay away from him and from the other one and focus on your future. Forget about the heroes and why they were here. Necsa is our leader, and you have to trust her to do the right thing."

"She's not, though. She wants to kill an innocent man. How can you allow that to happen?"

"Forget about all of that," Amyas's mother said. "Heroes are sneaky. They lied to you, and you shouldn't believe them. You should trust Necsa. She's our elected leader, and she knows what she's doing. She's going to punish you if she finds out you left the village. I don't want that or anything else to happen to you. It would ruin your possibilities of a good future and marriage."

Amyas should have known better. He wasn't sure he'd expected anything different, but he'd had to try.

He stepped closer to the front door. "I can't believe this. I know Necsa is our leader, but it doesn't mean she's perfect. If she were a good leader, she would listen to what her people have to say, and that includes me. If you're not going to help, I'm going to do it myself."

"The hero isn't a human. He won't give you a soul if you marry him," Amyas's mother said.

Amyas threw his hands in the air. "Why do you think that's the only thing I want in life? I don't care about souls. I don't *want* a soul. I also don't want the hero." Even though he was gorgeous.

But this wasn't about wanting a lover or someone to marry. Amyas didn't want to marry anyone, and he didn't *need* anyone, especially not a hero. It didn't matter that Mordred was reformed and helping instead of hurting supernatural creatures.

Amyas wanted to help Mordred because it was the right thing to do, and he hoped that Mordred would take him along when he left. As soon as he was away from the lake, Amyas would go his own way, and he and Mordred never had to see each other again.

But Mordred was Amyas's best way to get out of the situation.

"You have to stay out of this," Amyas's father repeated.

He was clearly scared. Amyas was, too, so he understood. He might not be close to his parents, but the thought of leaving them and everything he knew behind was terrifying. He was ready for it, though. His sister had left the village, and she'd only come back to tell them she was getting married to a human. Amyas wouldn't be doing the same, but he would still be leaving. It just wouldn't be the way his parents had expected him to.

He had to make a plan. He needed to talk to Mordred again and make sure Mordred would take him along when he left. That was his one condition, and he wouldn't help Mordred if he didn't agree.

Amyas frowned. Who was he trying to fool? Of course he would help Mordred regardless of what the hero decided to do with him. He couldn't allow Necsa to hurt someone who was there to help and who wouldn't be in this situation if they hadn't been trying to do that.

"Tell me you won't get involved," Amyas's father said.

He reached for Amyas again, but Amyas moved out of the way. His father's expression crumbled, but Amyas couldn't allow that to change his mind. Still, he was sure his parents would talk to Necsa if he told them what he was planning, so he forced himself to smile. "I will," he said.

His father blinked at him. "You'll stay away from the heroes?"

"Yes. I still think Necsa is making a mistake, but you're right. She's our leader, and I don't have a say in how she leads the village. This isn't my business."

Amyas's father looked like he couldn't quite believe what Amyas was saying, which wasn't surprising. Amyas wasn't known to give up or give in. He had to act like he was in this situation, but he normally wouldn't.

"I promise I won't do anything stupid," he said, trying to convince his father to believe him. "I don't like what's happening, but I'm only one person. I won't be able to change anyone's mind, and I don't want to be punished. I think the hero should be freed, but I won't sacrifice myself for someone I don't know. I'm sorry I made you worry. I thought you would help me, but since I'm the only one to think this way, maybe I'm wrong."

Amyas's father slowly nodded. "Good. I'm happy to see you understand."

"I do. I'm going to go to my room."

"We'll be here if you need us," Amyas's mother said.

Amyas didn't even look at her. He had to do something, and he didn't have a lot of time. Necsa wasn't going to keep the heroes there for much longer, not when she was planning to kill them.

Mordred had been waiting for Amyas to come back. He wasn't surprised to see him once the sun went down, but he *was* surprised at his own reaction to it. He was happy to see Amyas. Mostly, it was because he hoped Amyas would free him. In part, though, it was because he liked what he'd seen of Amyas so far.

It wasn't really physical. He didn't know Amyas, but the fact that the undine cared enough to bring him food had touched him. The way Amyas looked didn't have a lot to do with the situation, although Mordred had to admit he was pleasant to look at.

He watched as Amyas came out of the lake, water dripping around him. It was obvious from his stance that he was being careful and that he was afraid someone would catch him, which told Mordred that probably no one knew Amyas was here. He was going against his leader's will, which was impressive.

He moved closer to Mordred and Percival, and of course, Percival had to open his big mouth. "We don't want your food," he snapped.

Mordred almost laughed when Amyas answered. "I didn't bring you food. You can starve to death as far as I'm concerned. I'm not here for you anyway."

Percival spluttered, but Amyas had already dismissed him and turned his attention to Mordred. He stood over Mordred, and Mordred smiled at him. He had no idea why Amyas had come, but he hoped it was a good thing.

"I'll untie you," Amyas finally said.

"Thank you." Mordred could only imagine how hard it was for Amyas to do this. He supposed he had a similar experience, since he'd gone against the conclave's orders all those years ago. Still, Amyas was young. There was no way for Mordred to know how old he was, since undines were immortal until they married a human, but if Mordred had to guess, he hadn't been born a long time ago. He behaved like a young person, and Mordred suspected that was one of the reasons he'd believed him. The older undines obeyed their leader, but Amyas was young enough to rebel.

"I have a condition," Amyas continued.

Mordred wasn't surprised at that, either. "I'm listening."

"I want to go with you."

That was *not* what Mordred had expected, although he wasn't entirely surprised. "You're an undine. Why would you want to leave your life and your family?"

"Because I don't want to live here. I don't want to marry a human, and I don't want a soul. I don't care what everyone else wants for me. I want to be free."

Mordred didn't have to think about it. "I'll take you with me." He didn't know what would happen once they were gone, but they would have time to figure things out. Right now, the most important thing was to get out of here before Necsa and her warriors realized what was happening.

Amyas didn't waste any more time. He crouched next to Mordred, and Mordred felt something cut the ties that held him to the pole. Blood rushed to his hands, and he twisted his wrists this way and that, grimacing at the pinprick pain under his skin. By the time he was done, Amyas had untied his ankles, too, and Mordred rose to his feet.

"Help me, too," Percival said.

Amyas snorted. "Why should I? You made it obvious that you don't care about me and that you were here to kill my people. I should let Necsa kill you just like she intends to do."

"You should. It doesn't mean you're going to do it, though."

"I wouldn't be that arrogant if I were you," Mordred intervened. "You're at Amyas's mercy right now."

Percival glared, but Mordred must have gotten through, because he didn't say anything else. When he turned his gaze back to Amyas, he looked apologetic. "I shouldn't have acted the way I did. I thought you wanted to hurt me."

"Like the way you would have hurt my family and me?"

"You're supernatural creatures. You're dangerous."

"Which is why I should leave you here."

Mordred cleared his throat. "I'll free you," he told Percival.

He ignored Amyas's scandalized gaze and crouched next to the hero. He understood why Amyas didn't want to do this, but he had hope for Percival. Percival only knew what the conclave told him about supernatural creatures. Maybe now that he'd seen Amyas and had interacted with him, he'd understand. "I'll give you my number," he said.

"I don't want anything from you," Percival snapped.

"Still. I'll give it to you, and if you ever need it, use it. You don't have to stay with the conclave. You might be a hero, but you can do something else with your life."

Percival opened his mouth to answer, but just then, someone in the lake cried out.

They'd been noticed.

Mordred rushed through untying Percival, dismissing him as soon as he was free. By the time that was done, though, warriors had already started coming out of the lake. Amyas was freaking out, staring at them and trembling.

This was what Mordred's life had been like for hundreds of years, so he barely had to think about it before he acted. He grabbed Amyas's arm and pulled him closer, facing the warriors. He felt Percival run away, but he didn't spare the hero a glance.

"I have to create a portal," he told Amyas without looking at him.

"You won't have to," someone else said, and Mordred grinned in relief.

He turned to look at Haven and Dimitri. "You have impeccable timing."

"We actually arrived a few minutes ago, but we were watching you and the undine," Haven said. "I would have left Percival tied to the pole."

Mordred rolled his eyes, but now wasn't the time or the place to start bickering with Haven. He needed to focus on the situation, and with the warriors surrounding them, it wasn't easy.

He understood better why Amyas was helping him, but Amyas clearly hadn't expected to be found out. If he ever decided to come back, he would be shunned, or worse, killed. Mordred didn't want that to happen. He didn't want Amyas to lose his family, so he hooked an arm around Amyas's neck and pulled him against his body.

Amyas yelped, and Mordred hurried to say, "Go along with what I'm saying."

"What are you doing?" Amyas asked.

Mordred turned his attention to the warriors. "I'm taking him with me. If you want him to live, you'll let us go."

"You dare take one of my people hostage?" Necsa said as she rose from the lake. The warriors parted to let her pass.

"I wouldn't have done it if you'd freed me like I asked you. Now, you're going to let me go, or I'll hurt him."

"You said you were here to help us, yet you're willing to hurt someone to get away?"

"I'm willing to do a lot to survive." Mordred pulled Amyas even closer.

Just like he'd thought, Amyas was a lot shorter, and so slight that Mordred wouldn't have a problem hauling him up and dragging him along.

Mordred looked at Haven, who looked horrified, and Dimitri. "Open the portal," he snapped.

Dimitri pushed Haven, who finally snapped back into motion. He thrust his hand out and opened the portal, still staring at Mordred. Mordred didn't care what he thought, not at the moment. He would have time to explain later, when all of them were safe—including Amyas.

"Ready?" he murmured against Amyas's ear.

Amyas shuddered. "What are you doing?"

"I'm leaving, and you're coming with me."

"Let's go," Dimitri said.

Mordred turned and saw Haven had finally opened a portal. He grinned at Necsa, taking pleasure in knowing that he was getting away from her. He'd been trying to help, and while he couldn't hold it against her not to have accepted, he wanted her to know what she was giving up. "I'm part of a group of rogue heroes. We work against the conclave, which is why we were here. We were trying to help. I'm sorry you didn't appreciate that help."

Then, just like he'd planned, he hauled Amyas into his

arms and moved toward the portal. He stepped through as he listened to Necsa yelling and the warriors finally moving, but it was too late.

Mordred was free, and so was Amyas.

Mordred let go of Amyas as soon as they stepped out of the portal, and Amyas stumbled. Mordred was there, though, offering his arm. Amyas was torn between accepting the help and staying as far away from Mordred as he could.

Mordred had done what Amyas had asked of him. He'd taken him along when he'd left, and he'd done it while making sure that if Amyas ever wanted to go home, he wouldn't be blamed for freeing Mordred. Amyas was sure that Necsa would find a way to blame him anyway, but he was thankful. He wasn't sure what to do now, though.

He looked around, expecting them to be wherever Mordred lived and worked, but they were in the middle of a forest instead.

"I'll open another portal," the blond man who'd arrived with the leshy said.

"Open it directly to the house," Mordred answered.

He stepped closer to Amyas, and Amyas couldn't find it in himself to move away. Right now, Mordred was the only thing Amyas knew in this world. He didn't have anything anymore—not his home, not his family, not his village.

He didn't know where he would go from here, and it was soothing to know that Mordred was there, even though they didn't know each other.

"I can't believe you took him hostage," the blond hero said.

Mordred shook his head, but he was smiling. "Don't you see? I didn't. Amyas asked me to take him when I left, which is why I did what I did. This way, he can go back if he decides to." He paused and turned to Amyas. "Amyas, these are

Haven and Dimitri. As you know, Dimitri is a leshy."

Amyas nodded. He was wary of Haven, because Haven was a hero, but then, so was Mordred. Still, Amyas stepped closer to Dimitri, who smiled at him.

Amyas had never been away from the lake. His parents had pushed him to leave so he could find a human to marry, but he'd resisted. Now, he realized he shouldn't have. He could have left and never come back, and they wouldn't have known he'd run away. He wouldn't be in a situation in which he had no one to trust.

He wanted to trust Dimitri, but could he? Dimitri was close to Haven, which could mean either that Haven was a good person, or that they both were bad people. Once again, Amyas cursed his parents. They'd only prepared him to marry a human. He had no idea how to deal with the world outside of that, and he definitely wasn't about to get married to Dimitri or Haven. He wasn't about to get married to anyone, period.

"I took you with me," Mordred said, getting Amyas's attention back. "You're free now. You can go wherever you want."

Amyas didn't know where that was. He didn't want to be left alone, because he had no idea how to deal with the world or where to go, so he decided to use the fact that he'd freed Mordred as leverage. "I freed you. You would have been killed if I hadn't."

Mordred looked amused, but he nodded. "You're right."

Amyas really wasn't. Even if he hadn't freed Mordred, Mordred's friends would have. Haven had said they'd been there a while, watching. This was all Amyas had, though. "I need help," he confessed.

"What do you need help for?"

"I wanted to get away, and I did. I don't know what to do now, though. I've never been away from the lake."

Mordred stared for a moment before slowly nodding. "I

see. I can take you anywhere you want. We can find a lake for you or something like that."

Amyas wanted to say yes, but he was too afraid. He also didn't want to be alone. He'd never been, and the thought was scary. "I want to stay with you."

Mordred's eyes widened. He worried the piercing in his lower lip with his teeth for a moment, looking thoughtful.

Amyas tried not to stare, but it wasn't easy. Mordred looked like no one he knew. He'd found Mordred gorgeous when he'd seen him from afar, but now that they were close, Mordred was even more beautiful. His dark hair flopped in front of his dark eyes, and even though Amyas couldn't see much since it was dark, the moonlight was strong enough to glint on the various bits of metal embedded in Mordred's face.

How could Mordred be a warrior with so many piercings? Weren't they dangerous when he fought? Amyas counted one lip piercing, one in the eyebrow, one in the nose, and at least three in each ear. He found them fascinating, but they also puzzled him.

"I'm not sure you would like where we're going," Mordred finally said.

"Where is that?"

"As I told your leader, I'm part of a rogue heroes group. We all worked for the conclave once, but now we work against them. We try to save as many of their targets as we can. I'm always recruiting heroes, and most of us live together in the house. If you come with me, it means you'll be around many heroes, and I doubt you'd be comfortable there."

Mordred was probably right. Amyas couldn't see himself living with heroes, but he also couldn't see himself living alone. "What about Dimitri?"

Mordred looked at Haven, who was still glaring and keeping the new portal open, and Dimitri. "They don't live with us. They're not even part of the group. I've asked them to work with us, but they haven't given me an answer yet."

"We agree," Dimitri said. "We want to work with you and your people, and we'll move into the house."

Mordred blinked. "Are you sure? Because your boyfriend here doesn't look happy about that."

That was interesting. Amyas had thought that Dimitri and Haven worked together, but he hadn't realized they were actually a couple. It didn't make much sense, but then, nothing in this situation did. Maybe that was why Haven had stopped working for the conclave. He'd fallen in love with Dimitri and realized how wrong the conclave was.

Whatever had happened, it wasn't Amyas's business. He still hoped Dimitri and Haven would move into the house, though. He didn't want to be the only supernatural creature there, surrounded by heroes, rogue or not.

"We're sure," Haven said. "Can we go now? I don't want to stick around here for longer than we have to. I used an untraceable portal, but you never know. Since we're running both from the conclave and from Amyas's people, I don't want us to linger in the same place for too long, not without added protection."

Mordred looked at Amyas, who nodded. He was surprised when Mordred offered him his hand, but he took it. He didn't know Mordred, but he couldn't give him up.

He didn't want to.

Haven grabbed Dimitri and stepped through the portal. Mordred didn't follow him yet, though, looking at Amyas instead. "Ready?"

"Of course." It would only be the second time Amyas crossed a portal, and the last time, he hadn't had time to wrap his mind around what was happening. He hated not knowing what would be waiting for him on the other side, but he couldn't go back. He'd made his decision, and he didn't regret it, not yet anyway. He supposed there was more than enough time for him to start, but for now, he knew he'd made the right choice.

He'd helped free an innocent man, at least when it came to attacking his village. Mordred had only been trying to help, and now he would be able to help more supernatural creatures. As for Amyas, this was the start of his new life, a life he hadn't expected to have.

He might be terrified, but he also couldn't wait.

CHAPTER FOUR

"How are the chimeras settling down?" Mordred asked Bayard.

"As well as expected. They're not happy they had to leave their homes, but they understood why it was necessary."

"Have you heard anything about the undines?" It had been about a week since Amyas and Mordred had left them, and Mordred doubted the undines would sit back and forget about them. They couldn't get to Amyas here, but that didn't mean they wouldn't try, and it made Mordred nervous.

Bayard shook his head. "Nothing. You shouldn't worry about them. They can't find him."

Mordred nodded. "I know." But he was still worried. "Any news about the conclave?"

"I texted our contacts, and so far, everything is normal. The conclave is quiet, which is worrying."

The sound of singing distracted Mordred. He knew who it was without having to look out the window. Amyas had been singing his way around the house since he'd moved in, and Mordred loved it. He was also incredibly distracted by the singing and by Amyas in general.

He wasn't sure what to make of the undine. He liked Amyas, and he was protective of him, no doubt because Amyas had protected and freed him even though he shouldn't have. He'd sacrificed a lot for Mordred, and Mordred felt indebted to him. He wished he could do more, but Amyas had brushed off every attempt of Mordred to find him a new lake or village. He didn't want to have to live with other undines. Apparently, he was more than happy here, although Mordred found that hard to believe.

Bayard cleared his throat. Mordred snapped his gaze to his friend, not surprised to see Bayard looking amused. "You were saying?" he asked, trying to sound natural.

"That none of our contacts have anything to tell us. The conclave has been quiet, and no one is sure why."

"I'll try to contact the person I have in the conclave itself." Mordred didn't do that often, and not even Bayard or Eudocia knew who it was, but sometimes it was necessary. Mordred knew how much his contact was risking, so he had to be careful. They both did.

"You think they're planning something."

Mordred snorted. "When isn't the conclave planning something? We both know they are, and I want to know what it is before they do it. They know about us, and I doubt they'll sit back and allow us to continue doing what we've been doing. They can't find us yet, but they can certainly try, and they will."

Bayard nodded. "I'll make sure the security system is working as it should. I'll also tell everyone to keep an eye open, just in case."

"They should already know to keep an eye open."

"They do, but it bears repeating, and it's not like it's going to take much." Bayard paused, and his gaze glinted. It was enough for Mordred to know he wouldn't like whatever his second said next. "They shouldn't be distracted, and neither should you."

There it was. "I'm not distracted." But Mordred couldn't stop listening to Amyas singing, even now. Half of his attention was on Bayard, but the other half was definitely on Amyas.

Bayard arched a brow. "Really? Because to me, it looks like you've been distracted since you came back from the lake. I'm pretty sure it has a lot to do with a certain undine."

Mordred turned his gaze toward the documents on his desk. "I don't know what you're talking about."

Bayard's tone was softer when he next answered. "You know it's not a problem, right? No one is going to hold it against you if you want something with Amyas."

"There's nothing between Amyas and me. I'm a hero, and he doesn't like heroes."

"You're not just a hero, though. You took him away from his family, which was what he wanted."

"Only because they were suffocating him. I'm protecting him, just like he deserves. He sacrificed everything to help me. It doesn't mean I'm going to take advantage of it, or his gratitude."

Bayard frowned. "No one said you were going to take advantage. Amyas is more than able to say no if he doesn't want you, or to defend himself. Hasn't he been taking self-defense courses?"

Mordred blinked. "You mean the fighting lessons with Eudocia?"

"She had to modify them when he asked if he could participate, but yes. He's learning to defend himself. He's training with the other heroes, and even though they're going easy on him, he's doing well. Is it because he's a supernatural being?"

Mordred leaned back in his chair. It was hard to ignore Amyas's singing right now, even though Mordred was doing his best to focus on Bayard. "It has nothing to do with that, and you know it. I don't have a problem with supernatural beings. Otherwise, Dimitri and Amyas wouldn't be here."

"I know you don't care about that. I was just wondering if you thought we would care. All your relationships have been with heroes, but now, you like Amyas."

Mordred shook his head. "Not that way." He wasn't sure why he kept insisting on that, except for the fact that he couldn't do this to Amyas.

Amyas was here because he wanted to be free. Being involved with a hero would mean he couldn't leave, which Mordred suspected would happen sooner rather than later. Right now, Amyas wanted to stay because Mordred and the house were the only things he knew apart from the lake. He wanted to be free, but he was also clearly terrified at how big the world was. He didn't know much about it, but he was learning.

And eventually, he would go. He would settle down, live his own life, and Mordred would lose him. He couldn't afford to lose his heart, too, not when he had other things to think about. "I have to focus on work," he eventually said.

He was pretty sure Bayard wanted to roll his eyes, but thankfully, he didn't. "You can have a private life, too. You wouldn't be the only hero in a relationship. Having someone to love and who loves you doesn't mean you're distracted."

"This is the first time Amyas has a chance at whatever life he might want. I can't clip his wings that way. I don't want to complicate things, not when it comes to that, or when it comes to the heroes and how we live together. You know as well as I do that some people would be jealous and wouldn't like it if I got with him."

"If they were jealous, they would be assholes. Everyone wants you to be happy, Mordred. It doesn't matter who you're happy with."

Mordred playfully glared at Bayard. He wanted this conversation to end, but he didn't want to be rude. "Are we done talking about my private life? I'm not going to talk to Amyas about this, so you can stop pushing."

Bayard stared for a moment, then nodded. "All right. I just want to reiterate that no one here would care if you were with him. You might think some would be jealous, but most of us would be happy for you. You've been working a lot, helping people and supernatural beings for hundreds of years. No one would berate you for wanting a private life."

"Maybe once the conclave is gone."

Bayard shook his head. "They're never going to be gone, and you know it. Even if you take down every single conclave member, there will always be more. They won't ever disappear, but that's okay. We'll always be there to fight against them, and our ranks are growing. You need to start delegating, Mordred. It's why you have two seconds. Take some time off work and focus on your private life."

The problem with that was that Mordred would have to admit he didn't have a private life. Before meeting Amyas, he'd only been focused on work, and even though half of his mind was on Amyas now, he'd been doing his best not to let it show. Obviously, he'd failed. He couldn't help but wonder if Amyas had noticed, too, and what he thought about it if he had. Was this something he might want?

Mordred wouldn't find out if he didn't ask him, and he had no intention of doing that. He hadn't been lying when he'd said he didn't want to complicate things, neither for him nor for Amyas. If something was to develop between them, then it would, in time.

In the meantime, Mordred had work to do.

Amyas was in awe of the house. It was more like a palace, at least to him. The people who lived here didn't seem to notice, maybe because they'd been living here for a while. It was huge, and even after a week, Amyas was pretty sure he hadn't seen all of it.

He'd steered away from the private bedrooms as he'd explored, but he was curious. Were they all like his? He couldn't believe how much space he had just for himself. When he'd lived in the village, he'd shared his little house with his parents and his sister, when she still lived with them. It was what families usually did. A lot of younger undines left, married humans and never came back. Amyas and his sister had been supposed to do the same, and she had.

Amyas hadn't found a human to marry, but he'd left the village. Now, his parents were alone in the house, and he couldn't help but wonder if they thought about him. Were they worried? Or did they know he'd gone with Mordred because he'd wanted to?

Amyas couldn't believe Necsa had fallen for it. He hadn't even thought about doing something like that, and he'd been stunned when Mordred had acted as if he was taking him hostage. Amyas supposed it gave him the opportunity to go back to the village if he ever wanted to, although he doubted that would happen.

He was free.

Some people would think he'd exchanged one jail for another. He wasn't in the village anymore, but he hadn't left the house yet. He didn't feel like a prisoner, though. He had a lot of space to roam, both inside the house and outside. They were in a forest, and even though there was no lake nearby, Amyas was pretty sure he'd heard Mordred grumble about having one dug up.

He had no idea what to think about that.

He'd told himself this was going to be temporary, that as soon as he got his feet under him, he would go. He didn't know where, but that had been his plan. Now, he was changing his mind.

He didn't want to leave this place. It wasn't a prison. No one had expectations, and everyone was nice. Even when he asked for something stupid, they listened to him, like participating in the fighting lessons. He'd expected to get his ass beaten, and he had, but once he'd finished, Eudocia had come to him and told him she wanted to help him. He ought to be able to defend himself if he was ever going to leave and be on his own.

He'd never imagined something like this place could exist. He'd known how small his life had been, but now, he understood it even more. His parents had kept him in the village, had insisted that his only way to get out was to marry a human. He hadn't, yet he was free. He intended to stay that way, even though he felt guilty about leaving his family behind.

He continued singing as he walked through rooms he knew by heart now. They were all beautiful, and they reminded him of home in a way. There was a lot of stone, but here, the coldness of it was offset by the softness of tapestries and carpets. Amyas could walk barefoot around the house, and he would be warm the entire time.

He didn't want to stay inside. He wanted a breath of fresh air, and since the sun was shining, he headed toward the back of the house. When he opened the door, he closed his eyes and stood still, basking in the sunlight. He missed being able to swim in the lake, but apart from that, he was happier than he'd ever been.

He stepped outside and closed the door behind himself. The house was big, but it was nothing next to how big the outside property was. Amyas could explore it for days and not see all of it, even though he'd been trying.

He headed toward his favorite spot — it was hidden, with a small fountain and stone benches. It was the closest thing he had to a body of water, and for now, he was more than happy with it.

It was usually empty, but today, it wasn't. Dimitri was sitting on the bench, his legs crossed under him, a smile on his face, and his eyes closed. Amyas hesitated. He wondered if Dimitri was there because he wanted some time alone, and if that was the case, whether Amyas should go back to the house or find another spot to spend time in.

He wasn't quite sure how to behave when it came to Dimitri. Undines were used to dealing with other elemental creatures, and that included leshy. It had never been Amyas's job, though. Even though he'd seen leshy and undines work together and had even talked to a few, they'd always felt strange. Everything felt strange these days, though, so he supposed he should just see what would happen.

"Amyas. You can sit with me," Dimitri said when he opened his eyes and noticed him.

Amyas supposed that solved his problem. "Thank you. I don't want to bother you."

"You're not bothering me. I needed some time in nature, and I love that this place has such beautiful spots on the property."

Amyas sat on one of the other stone benches. "This is one of my favorite spots, although I haven't explored everything yet."

"It's huge, isn't it?"

"Especially compared to the village I lived in before. I never imagined something like this existed."

Dimitri looked at Amyas. "It has to be overwhelming for you."

"It is, but in the best of ways. It's a lot to take in, but being here means I'm free."

Dimitri's smile was gentle. "I understand. I know a bit about undines, but I've never actually worked with any."

"How come? The village works with several leshies."

Dimitri shrugged one shoulder. "I've never been like most leshy. I have the same powers, of course, but I've been using them in different ways. I usually work alone."

"I thought you and Haven had been together a while."

Dimitri shook his head. "Not long, no. He was a surprise. I thought I'd continue working on my own, but instead, here I am. Sometimes it's still confusing, but I wouldn't stop for anything in the world. Even though I know my work before was good, I was alone. I'm not anymore, and even though I never knew I wanted this, I'm happy I found it. It's so much better and easier to work when someone has your back."

"You're a fighter. You work with the heroes. I'm not sure what *I'm* doing here."

"Anything you want to do."

"I don't know what I want to do." Amyas raised his feet and pressed them onto the bench, hugging his knees close to his chest. "All my life, I was told that my main goal was supposed to be finding a human to marry."

Dimitri nodded. "So you could get a soul."

"Yes. It's what every undine wants."

"Apparently, not all of them. From the way you're talking, I doubt it's something you've ever wanted."

"It's not. I don't want to marry anyone, least of all to have a soul. I don't *need* anyone, not that way."

"It doesn't mean you shouldn't have someone that way."

Amyas frowned. He couldn't say he'd never thought about it, but it hadn't been a priority. Could he truly find someone to share his life with? Someone who wasn't a human, who Amyas wouldn't marry just to get a soul? "How did you and Haven meet?" he asked.

Dimitri's smile widened. "He was sent by the conclave to kill me."

Amyas gaped. "Are you serious?"

"Very much so. If you have time, I can tell you the story."

Amyas grinned. "I have nothing but time right now."

"Good. Now, Haven worked for the conclave until recently," Dimitri began.

Amyas settled in to listen. Maybe knowing Dimitri's story would help him decide what to do next with his life, and even if it didn't, Amyas could use a friend.

Chapter Five

Mordred had always loved having dinner with the former conclave heroes. It was the perfect time for them to talk, to establish bonds that went beyond what they were born as. It was always awkward when they recruited new heroes, but they usually fit in well, even those who chose not to live at the house. Mordred insisted on this kind of dinner at least once a month, and they were even more interesting now with Dimitri and Amyas there.

Mordred couldn't seem to look away from Amyas. He'd been at the house for almost two weeks now, and he'd settled in perfectly, better than Mordred had expected. Just like he'd thought, the heroes had welcomed both Amyas and Dimitri. A few were wary, no doubt because of how often the conclave had told them that supernatural beings were monsters, but they believed in the cause, even if it was taking them some time to warm up to having two supernatural beings living with them.

All in all, everything was going well, even though the conclave was being quiet, which worried Mordred. He couldn't seem to focus on that for any length of time, though. His gaze kept slipping to Amyas, who was sitting with Dimitri and Haven. Mordred couldn't tell whether or not Haven was happy about it. His expression was neutral, although every time Dimitri talked to him, he smiled. It transformed him, and Mordred understood better why Haven had decided to leave the conclave behind.

"You're staring again," Bayard said.

Mordred did his best not to scowl at him, but he was pretty sure he failed, given the way Eudocia arched a brow.

"What are you two talking about?" she asked.

"Nothing," Mordred hurried to say.

Bayard wasn't going to just forget about this, though. "I think he's in love with Amyas," he told Eudocia.

To Mordred's surprise, she grinned. "I thought I saw something there. I'm not surprised. Amyas is a great guy."

Mordred huffed. "Are you done talking about me as if I'm not even here? I already told you, Bay, there's nothing between Amyas and me."

"Yet. It doesn't mean there can't be anything."

"I haven't changed my mind. I want to give Amyas as much freedom as possible, especially since he's stuck in this house. He left his village because it was too restrictive, and I don't want to make the same mistake."

"I don't think he feels restricted," Eudocia said. "Of course, I don't know him well, but we've talked several times. He always stays after the fighting lessons, and he's great. I'm not surprised you're interested in him, Mordred."

"I'm not. Haven't the two of you heard what I just said? Amyas is here because he didn't want to be forced into marriage with a human. I doubt that being with a hero is on his list of priorities. Besides, I'm way too busy, and my work is dangerous. Why would I subject Amyas to that? He could have anyone he wants. Why would he settle for me?"

Eudocia reached behind Mordred and slapped the back of his head. Mordred spluttered, glaring at her, but she just glared back.

"Are you done?" she asked.

"What did you do that for?"

"I did it because you're being an idiot, although I'm not surprised. Men generally are, and it doesn't matter if they're immortal, obviously."

"Will you stop that? I don't know why the two of you decided that you have to play matchmakers, but please, don't."

"We're not playing matchmakers. We just see what's in front of our eyes, and apparently, you don't. You're a catch, Mordred." Eudocia sounded sure of that.

Mordred snorted. He knew he was good-looking and that he had a good body, but that didn't make him a good catch. "I'm a rogue hero. I might have been away from the conclave for two hundred years, but I still worked for them for too long. How could anyone like Amyas want to be with me? And even if he could overlook that and the fact that I killed numerous innocent people, why would he want to be with someone who could die any day?"

"You *are* aware that killing heroes isn't that easy, right?" Bayard asked as if he thought Mordred was stupid.

"I am. It doesn't mean we don't sometimes lose a hero. And even if I'm not killed, I could be maimed. What we do is dangerous, even though it's the right thing to do. If Amyas ever wants someone in his life, he should look at people who aren't in danger every day and who wouldn't be putting him in danger just by living."

"So you think none of us should have someone in their life?" Eudocia asked.

"That's not what I said."

"It is, though. Our lives are dangerous, and there's no getting out of it, not unless you want to stop, and I don't. It doesn't mean I plan on spending the rest of eternity on my own, though. What we do comes with risks, but as long as the person we're with knows that, I don't see why being with them should be a problem. That includes Amyas. You say that you want him to have a choice, but you're not giving him one, not when it comes to this."

Mordred shook his head and got to his feet. "I'm done talking about this."

"So you're going to run away?"

He glared at Eudocia. Right now, he couldn't remember why he'd chosen her as his second. She was annoying, and he didn't want to talk about this anymore. "I'm not running away. The two of you won't listen to what I'm saying, and I don't want to have to repeat myself. Being with someone might be right for you, but it doesn't mean it's right for everyone, and you know nothing about how I feel."

Eudocia's expression twisted. "Maybe not. But Bayard and me, and everyone else here, have been watching you working yourself to the bone for the past two hundred years. When was the last time you took a day off?"

"There's no time to take a day off." Mordred and the conversation he was having with his seconds was drawing attention, and that was the last thing he wanted. "I'm going to my office. I have some work to do before I can go to bed."

"That's what I was talking about," Eudocia pointed out, but Mordred didn't want to listen to this anymore. He left the dining room, patting a few people on the shoulders and smiling at them without stopping as he went. He didn't look at Amyas again on purpose, not wanting to want to stay.

Then he stumbled onto Amyas just outside the dining room.

"What are you doing here?" he asked before he could think better of it.

Amyas cocked his head. "I was going back to the dining room. What are *you* doing?"

"I'm going to my office. I have work to do."

"Work?" Amyas frowned. "It's late in the evening. I thought you were having fun?"

"I was, but my work comes with long hours."

"So long that you can't take the time to have dinner with your family?"

Mordred rubbed the back of his neck. Amyas always took

him by surprise, and he never knew how to behave with him. "The heroes aren't my family, even though we share the house."

"Are you sure? What's a family for you? Is it only connected by blood, or is there more?"

Mordred did *not* want to talk about this right now, but he couldn't just leave. "A family is people who care about each other and love each other. People who are there for each other through thick and thin. It's chosen, and it doesn't have anything to do with blood."

Amyas looked victorious. "See? That's what I was talking about. You just described yourself and your heroes. You might not be as close to all of them as you could be, but it doesn't mean they're not part of your family. They're just distant cousins or something like that. But I saw you with Bayard and Eudocia. You love them."

"They're my seconds."

Amyas narrowed his eyes. "They are, but it doesn't mean you don't love them. It doesn't mean they're not your family."

Amyas shouldn't find Mordred adorable. Mordred was too big and strong to be adorable, but when he was flustered like he was now, it made Amyas's heart soften. He couldn't help but wonder what it would be like to be with Mordred. He'd seen how Mordred behaved with his friends, with the people he considered family, even though he didn't want to admit it. He cared about them and always made sure they were happy, safe, and had everything they might want. They worked together, but Mordred was undeniably the head of the family, the person everyone looked up to.

That included Amyas. He wasn't sure when it had happened — maybe the first time he and Mordred had met, or maybe when Mordred had agreed to take Amyas along when he left. The *when* didn't matter. Amyas had come to see Mordred as a person who cared for him and a person he cared about, too.

That didn't change the fact that he and Mordred couldn't be together. Amyas didn't need anyone. He didn't need a human to get a soul — or a man in general. Still, his growing feelings for Mordred made him think.

He didn't want to get married to gain a soul and lose his immortality, but could he really be alone for the rest of his life? From what he'd gleaned from his conversation with Eudocia, that was what Mordred was doing. Eudocia had told Amyas that while Mordred had relationships every so often, they never lasted long, and it was obvious to everyone that even though Mordred cared for the people he was with, he wasn't in love with them. He kept them at arm's length, and Amyas wanted to know why.

Eternity sounded great, but not when it was spent alone.

"Maybe you're right," Mordred said.

Amyas had allowed his thoughts to distract him, but he came back to the conversation. "I know I am. All the people in the dining room are your family, whether or not you like that idea. They look up to you as if you were a father."

Mordred grimaced. "I don't want to be Eudocia or Bayard's father. That's just strange."

Amyas shook his head, amused. "A father figure, then. You know what I mean. These people admire you. They're here for that reason."

"They're here because they know the conclave is wrong, and they want to do something about it."

"Maybe, in part. They don't have to be part of another organization to do that, though. If I was a hero, I wouldn't want to go anywhere near another one after what happened with the conclave. But your people trust you, and they're here because of that. I have no doubt they want to help supernatural beings and to stop the conclave, but that's not all there is to it." And Amyas didn't understand why Mordred couldn't see that.

Mordred looked strong, but Amyas was starting to understand that inside, he might be fragile. He knew what to do when it came to fighting and protecting people, but had anyone ever protected *him*? Amyas wanted to be that person, but he knew better than to do anything about it right now. He was too confused, and he needed to think and make decisions before he could allow anything to happen between him and Mordred. Besides, he didn't know what Mordred thought of him or if he could want something like this. It might be wishful thinking, and then Amyas would make a fool of himself.

Mordred wouldn't kick Amyas out for trying to kiss him or something like that, but he still didn't have the guts to do it, not when he didn't know what he wanted his future to be like.

"You should go back to dinner," Mordred said.

"While you go back to your office?"

"I have work to do."

"Why do you work so much?"

"I do what I have to do to protect people."

From Mordred's expression, Amyas could tell he was telling the truth. He truly thought that he had to work all the time to protect people, and maybe he wasn't wrong. Maybe he was, though. "Has anyone contacted you about the conclave targeting supernatural beings?"

"Not today. The conclave has been incredibly quiet lately, which is worrying."

Amyas nodded. "I agree it is, but is there anything you can do right now?"

"No. I have to wait for the conclave to take the next step. I don't know where they're going to be or why."

"Then maybe you could relax, at least for one evening? I

know you feel like if you're not in control all the time, people are going to get hurt, but you're wrong. Besides, even if it does happen, you're doing everything you can. No one would blame you for taking a day off, or even a *week* off."

Mordred looked horrified at the thought, which made Amyas chuckle. He truly was high strung, wasn't he?

"I can't take a week off," Mordred protested.

"Not a week, then. The evening?"

Mordred looked back at the dining room. They could both hear people inside, talking and laughing. They even *sounded* like a family, and Amyas didn't understand how Mordred hadn't seen that sooner. It shouldn't have taken Amyas to point it out.

"I can't go back, not when I told everyone I was going to work."

"I don't think anyone would care. They know how important the job is to you, and no one would hold it against you if you relax for a bit. But I doubt I'm the only one who told you that, yet you don't seem to listen."

Mordred pushed his hands into his pockets and shrugged. He looked younger when he did things like that, and that made Amyas wants to step closer and hug him.

"I suppose you could say I'm stubborn," Mordred admitted.

Amyas snorted. "That's an understatement. I like you stubborn, though."

Mordred's eyes widened for a moment, but he quickly schooled his expression.

Amyas was sorry. He wanted Mordred to know he didn't have to act like he didn't care, not with him.

"You like me?" Mordred asked.

"Probably more than I should, considering the situation. I don't think anyone could *not* like you, though. You're a good person, no matter what you seem to think."

"I never said I wasn't a good person."

"But you don't feel like you deserve time off work. You don't feel like you deserve a family. To me, that's telling."

Mordred looked like he wanted to protest, but just then, someone stepped out of the dining room. The hero froze when she saw Mordred and Amyas there, and she quickly stepped back into the room, but it was too late. Whatever had been going on between Amyas and Mordred was gone. Mordred shuffled his feet and tilted his chin toward the end of the hallway. "I really should go. And you should go back to the dining room. I'm sure your friends are waiting for you."

"They're your friends, too."

"Maybe. They know I have work to do, though. This mission is important for all of us, and I have to focus on it."

Amyas wanted to ask him what was more important — the mission, or possibly him — but he didn't dare, not when he didn't know what he wanted himself.

Eventually, he would, though. When that happened, he would finally be able to make a decision about Mordred. He wanted Mordred to be free, just like he was, and while he might not be behind bars, it was obvious he'd kept himself apart from the other heroes. He carried a lot of weight on his shoulders, and to Amyas's own surprise, he wanted to shoulder some of it. He wanted to make Mordred's life easier since he was helping so many people, but he didn't know where to start.

He supposed he was going to have to think about that, too, and he had all the time in the world, since he wasn't giving up his immortality anytime soon.

CHAPTER SIX

Amyas bit his lower lip. He knew he needed to do this, but he was afraid. What would his parents say? He hadn't heard from them since he'd left the lake, and they had to be worried. They would probably be happy to hear from him, but as soon as he told them what had happened and what he was doing, they would be angry. He didn't want to lose them, but he also didn't want to lose his newfound freedom. Still, they were his parents. They'd raised him, and he felt like he owed it to them to at least tell them he was okay. He didn't want them to think Mordred was a monster, even though Mordred had been the one who acted as if he was taking Amyas as a hostage. Amyas wanted everyone to know that Mordred was a good person, though, and the only way to do that was to talk to his parents.

He hoped they would forgive him once he told them what he'd done, but even if they didn't, he wanted them to know he was okay. He felt like once he did this, he would be readier to make decisions about his future. He'd been trying to think for weeks now, and so far, he hadn't come up with anything.

He wasn't in a rush. Mordred had made sure to tell him that, and he wasn't lying. He wasn't the kind of person who would do something like that, especially not to Amyas. But Amyas had to make a decision, and he had to move forward. His parents and what they thought of him were holding him back, which meant he had to make some changes.

He looked at the bowl he'd snuck out of the kitchen. He could have asked to borrow it, but he didn't want to have to explain why he wanted it. He doubted Mordred would forbid him to contact his family, but he still felt like it was something he shouldn't be doing, and he wanted it to be private. If anything weird happened, he would tell Mordred. Otherwise, he didn't see why he should.

Amyas went to his private bathroom and filled the bowl. Then he went back to his bedroom, put it onto one of the nightstands, and sat on the bed with his legs crossed. He took a few moments to breathe and gather his thoughts. This wasn't going to be easy, but if he didn't do it now, he never would. He might as well get it out of the way.

He took the bowl from the nightstand, settled it on top of his crossed legs, and took a deep breath. He closed his eyes, almost losing his cool, but he forced himself to go through the motions of using the water as a way to communicate. That was how they did things in the lake, or at least, how Necsa contacted other undines and supernatural beings. Amyas had never had a reason to contact anyone this way, since he'd never left the lake, not until Mordred had taken him away.

With another deep breath, Amyas opened the communication with his parents. The first thing he saw was the living room of the home he'd grown up in. His parents were there. He sucked in a breath. It was enough to get his mother's attention, and she looked up.

Amyas wasn't sure what she saw, but he knew it had to be his face. She gasped and brought a hand to her mouth, never looking away. Amyas's father noticed, and he looked up, too. His eyes widened and he jumped to his feet, reaching for Amyas. He couldn't touch him, though, and Amyas felt a twinge of pain and guilt at the thought.

Was he doing the right thing, or would a clean break have been better? Whatever the answer, it was too late to change his mind.

"Hi," he said.

"Amyas! We thought you were dead. We thought the heroes had killed you."

Amyas frowned, although he understood why his parents might think that. "I told you the heroes wouldn't hurt me."

"He took you away from us. How were we supposed to know he wouldn't hurt you?"

"Well, you can stop worrying about that. I'm fine."

"Are you coming home?"

Amyas hesitated. He didn't want to tell his parents the truth. He was afraid that if he ever wanted to go home, he wouldn't be able to.

But he'd made his decision. He was staying away, and if that meant permanently losing his home, that was fine. He'd build a new home somewhere, with a new family.

"I'm not. I'm sorry. I promise you I'm fine, but I'm never coming back."

Amyas's father shook his head. "Where are you? We can pick you up."

"Dad. You have to listen to me, please. Mordred didn't take me hostage. He did what he did because I asked him to take me along when he left, and he wanted me to be able to go home if I decided to. He hasn't mistreated me, and I trust him."

"You went with him willingly?" Amyas's mother asked.

Amyas nodded. "I did. I wanted out, and I untied him."

"How could you do something like that? Necsa and everyone else in the village has been looking for you for weeks. We thought you were dead, that the heroes had hurt you. Instead, you went there of your own accord?"

"I know you're angry—"

"Angry? We're not angry, Amyas. It's more than that. Why did you do it? Are you and that hero together? He's not a human, and he won't give you a soul. You can't marry him."

Amyas rolled his eyes. *Of course* that was what his mother

thought about.

"Don't roll your eyes at me," she snapped.

Amyas didn't feel sorry. "Why shouldn't I, when you're saying something that stupid?"

She gasped, clearly not used to Amyas standing up to her.

He was done living the life his parents wanted him to live, though. Still, he probably shouldn't antagonize her or his father. Even if he never went home, he might be able to contact them the way he was now.

He swallowed and tried to focus on what he'd been planning to tell them. "I'm not with Mordred." Not yet anyway, but he wasn't about to admit to any of that. "We weren't together when I freed him, either. I'd never met him before that day. I did what I thought was the right thing to do. He and his people are only trying to help supernatural beings, and they were there to fight the other two heroes. Necsa never listened to me when I tried telling her, but I hope you will."

"You can't ask us to go against our leader," Amyas's father said.

"I'm not. I understand why you don't want to, but I'm your son."

"She's our leader. She has the experience you don't. Look at what happened. You freed the hero, and you went with him. You gave up everything me and your mother have been working for."

"Don't you see?" Amyas asked. He desperately needed his parents to understand. "I've never wanted the life you wanted for me. I don't want to marry a human. I don't want a soul. I want to be myself and do what I want, not what I'm supposed to want. I'm sorry if that disappoints you, and I'm sorry if you never want to talk to me again. I hope that won't be the case, but if it is, I'll respect your wish. I won't contact you again." Even though it broke his heart. He'd known what he was giving up when he'd decided to go with Mordred, though. He couldn't regret it.

"You need to give us time," Amyas's father said. "This is a lot for us to take in and to try to understand."

Amyas had suspected things would end like this, but it hurt. Still, it was better than his parents telling him they never wanted to hear from him again. "I'll give you that time, then."

"Are you sure you're safe?" his mother asked.

Amyas couldn't help but smile. "I'm sure. I know you don't have a reason to trust Mordred, but I do. He'll keep me safe, whatever happens." If there was one thing Amyas was sure of in this situation, it was that. Mordred would make sure nothing happened to him. Whatever Amyas decided, Mordred would be there for him and help him.

Even if Amyas decided to leave.

Mordred was upside down when he noticed Amyas walking toward the forest that framed the house. He straightened from his downward-facing dog position, frowning. It could be that Amyas hadn't noticed him, but he hadn't stopped to say hello. It was strange, because Amyas was always eager to talk to people, especially Mordred. Mordred thought about calling him over, but maybe he should go after him and see what happened instead. It was tempting, especially after the conversations he'd had with Bayard and Eudocia.

They wanted Mordred to be happy, and so did Mordred.

He should finish his yoga session, but this felt more important. If Amyas was in trouble, he needed someone, and that someone could be Mordred. He decided yoga could wait and quickly pushed his bare feet into his shoes. Then he followed Amyas into the forest.

The forest was one of the reasons he'd bought this house. It was isolated, which was perfect for what they did, and there was a lot of space to roam. They didn't need it, but it was always nice to have space when you were closed in a house with a bunch of other people most of the day. That was why the vast property was such a good thing. It gave everyone the space they needed, especially Amyas and Dimitri. Mordred knew they'd already taken advantage of it, and he hoped they would continue. He hoped they would come to consider this place their home, just like he did.

When he found Amyas, he was sitting on a stone bench with his legs stretched out and his feet resting in the small fountain that stood in front of the bench.

That was something Mordred should have thought of. Of course Amyas would need water. He was an undine. The only water he could get in the house was in the bathtub in his bathroom, but it wasn't good enough. Amyas deserved more, and Mordred would have to find a way to get that to him.

"Amyas?" he called out.

Amyas turned and smiled. He didn't look surprised to see Mordred. "I didn't want to bother you while you were training."

"You didn't."

"When I walked past you, I saw that you were in a strange position."

"I was doing yoga."

Amyas frowned. "Yoga?"

"I'll show you if you're interested, but that's not why I'm here."

"Why are you then?"

"Can I sit?"

Mordred wasn't sure what Amyas would think of him butting into his personal life. They'd talked before, and Amyas hadn't had a problem telling Mordred what he thought, but the same might not go the other way around.

But Amyas smiled and nodded. "Of course. This is your home, after all."

"It's your home, too. You don't have to let me sit if you don't want me to. I won't be offended."

"Maybe not, but I do want you to sit down." Amyas hesitated. "Especially if we're going to talk."

"Do you think we need to?"

Amyas sighed. "Probably. I did something stupid today."

Mordred couldn't think of a single thing Amyas might have done, especially not since he hadn't left the house. "I'm sure you're exaggerating."

"Not really." Amyas took a breath. "I contacted my parents."

Mordred wasn't surprised, although he was curious to find out how Amyas had managed. "I expected you to do that eventually."

Amyas frowned. "I put your people in danger, though."

"I wouldn't say that. Did you tell your parents where we are?"

"Of course not."

"Then they won't be able to find us. Don't worry too much. When I bought the house, I hired several witches and mages to put protective spells on the property. No one can find us, not the conclave, and not Necsa. You're safe, and so is everyone else."

That seemed to do the trick. Amyas's shoulders relaxed, and while he still didn't look happy, at least he wasn't beating himself up for contacting his parents.

"Do you want to talk about it?" Mordred asked.

Amyas sighed. "Not really, but I suppose I might as well."

"You don't have to do anything you don't want to do, Amyas."

"The problem is that I don't know what I want." Amyas sighed and rubbed his face with both his hands. "I was hoping that my parents were missing me. And maybe they are. I don't know. I wanted to reassure them I was okay, and I told them that you didn't really take me as a hostage. I explained you did it for my benefit, so I would be able to go home if I decided to. They were angry, but I suppose they would have forgiven me if I'd actually gone home."

"But you're not."

"I don't know. Maybe I should. Maybe the lake truly is the only place where I belong. They told me that being with you would be worthless to me, since it won't give me a soul."

Mordred swallowed. This wasn't where he'd expected the conversation to go, but he supposed that since it was, he might as well roll with it. "They think you want to be with me?"

"It's weird. They don't see much use for undines unless they have a soul. That means we have to marry a human like my sister did."

"But you don't want that." Mordred knew enough about Amyas to be sure of it.

"I never did. I don't care about having a soul. I don't want to tie my life and happiness to a person I don't know, least of all a human. You know that if my sister's husband cheats on her, she'll lose her soul again? Unless she has a child first, which I'm sure she's already trying to do. But it's not fair. Why should we depend on humans that way? And since we're born without a soul, why should we gain one? I'm not bad, and I'm no different from any other person, even though I don't have a soul."

Mordred agreed. He also understood that it was a sore subject for a lot of undines, including Amyas. "What did your parents say?"

"They ordered me to come home. They told me it was the only thing I could do and that I should find a human and marry them. It's what they always say. I don't even have the excuse that I'd rather marry a male anymore. Humans can do that now, so it wouldn't be a problem."

"But you don't want to do it."

Amyas shook his head. He looked miserable, and Mordred wished there was more he could do for him. Hopefully, listening to him and giving him advice would be enough.

"I don't know what I want to do. That's the problem. All my life, I've been told that my only goal should be finding a human and marrying them. Possibly having children, although since I wouldn't be the one carrying the kid, it wouldn't shield me from losing my soul if my human cheated on me. I'm an undine. It's what I'm supposed to do."

"*Supposed*. What do you actually want to do, though?"

Amyas shook his head. "I don't know."

"And this is why you left. Not being with your parents in the village gives you the chance to find out what you want to do with your life. You don't have to do it now. I had no idea what I was doing when I left the conclave, but I built something new, and I'm proud of it."

That got Amyas's attention. "What happened? Why did you leave?"

Mordred looked away from Amyas, staring at the trees instead. "I was with the conclave for more than six hundred years. For most of that time, I blindly believed everything they told me. I don't think I'll ever be able to atone for that and for all the supernatural beings I killed during that time. The conclave wasn't always as bad as they are now, though. In the beginning, they truly wanted to help humanity. It slowly changed, and I didn't notice."

Amyas reached for Mordred's hand, and Mordred watched as he took it. He couldn't have stopped Amyas even if he'd wanted to. He needed the contact and to feel like he wasn't alone. He never was, not truly, not in a home he shared with so many people, but this was different.

Amyas gently squeezed, and Mordred found the strength to continue. It wasn't easy to confess his sins to someone he liked, but he felt he had to. Maybe this would show Amyas that he could do anything he wanted in his life. "I started questioning the conclave's orders. I'm not even sure why. I suppose I saw too many innocent beings being killed, and I didn't understand why. It took me years to finally wrap my mind around what the conclave was doing and decide to do something about it. When I did, I knew I couldn't talk to any of them. They would have killed me, just like they had killed other people who had tried asking for explanations. They need to keep their authority over the heroes because, without them, the conclave is nothing. I couldn't ask questions, so one day, I just never went back after a mission. I didn't even complete that mission. I couldn't kill more innocents. I had money, so I bought this house. It took me a long time to decide what I wanted to do, and more lives were lost during that time."

"You're making up for it, though."

Mordred forced himself to look at Amyas. "I'm trying."

Amyas was fascinated. He wanted to know more about Mordred and his life, but he could tell pushing wouldn't help. Mordred would tell him when he was ready, and not one second sooner.

That was okay. Amyas wasn't going anywhere, so he and Mordred had time to get to know each other.

He was sad, but he wasn't tempted to go back to the lake. He knew what was waiting for him if he went, and that was the last thing he wanted.

He didn't want to find a human and get married. He *did* want to get to know Mordred better and see what might happen between them, though. He didn't care that Mordred was immortal and wouldn't be able to give him a soul. Amyas didn't need a soul.

He couldn't help but imagine what his life would be if he stayed here. Both he and Mordred had been talking as if it was temporary until Amyas got back on his feet, but Amyas found that he didn't want to leave. He liked living with the heroes. He liked being free to do what he wanted.

He liked *Mordred*.

Maybe he could work with Mordred and the heroes and help people. Dimitri was doing that, and while Amyas wasn't a fighter yet, he had an immortal life to learn and do what he could. No one would try to force him to do anything here, not even Mordred—maybe especially not him. It was strange to know that, but also freeing, even though Amyas was still hurting over what his parents had said.

He needed to get over it. He'd known what their reaction would be, even though he'd hoped for a different one. He had to stop thinking about that and about them, and focus on what he would do next.

No one would choose anything for him, and that included who he should be with.

He wasn't surprised that once again, the answer to that was Mordred. He had a bit of a crush on Mordred, and he'd had it since he'd first seen Mordred at the lake. He wouldn't say that was the reason he'd saved Mordred, but it certainly helped that he liked the man. He wasn't sure what he could do about it, and maybe the answer to that was nothing.

Maybe it wasn't, though.

Amyas was safe. Mordred would never hurt him, and he wanted more. He wanted to feel closer to someone, and if that someone was Mordred, well, it wasn't a problem.

Amyas got his feet out of the fountain, shook them to get the water off, and slid closer to Mordred on the bench.

Mordred smiled, but he didn't say anything. Instead, he allowed Amyas to move at his own pace, even though Amyas himself didn't know what that pace was.

Amyas stopped once his side brushed against Mordred's.

"Thank you," he murmured.

"There's nothing to thank me for."

"There is. I was sad, and I still am, but I feel better because I talked to you. You're right. I have to look at all the sides of the situation, and the most important thing is that now, I have a choice. I don't have to do what my parents expect from me. I don't have to find a human to marry or gain a soul. You put things into perspective for me. You went through so much, while I only had to tell my parents to leave me alone when it comes to marriage. My worries probably sound silly to you."

"They don't. Everyone has different worries, and that's fine. Life would be boring if we all had the same things to worry about."

"Maybe. I still find this world strange. I'm not used to any of this."

"And you don't have to be used to it. You don't have to rush into anything. I'm not your parents, Amyas, and I don't expect anything from you except for you to try your best to be happy, whatever that means."

"You sound too good to be true."

Mordred laughed. "I'm not. Some people will tell you I'm horrible."

Amyas frowned. "They would be wrong. You're not. You gave me an opportunity no one else would have given me."

"I think you would have made your way out of the lake, eventually."

Amyas wasn't too sure about that. He wanted to believe Mordred, but he knew himself. No matter how much he'd been against obeying his parents to find a human to marry, he thought that maybe eventually, he would have. He would have wanted to keep the peace with his parents and with Necsa. That would have been the only way to make that happen.

But not anymore. Thanks to Mordred, Amyas was making his own choices.

Amyas leaned his head against Mordred's shoulder, holding his breath. He didn't know how Mordred would react to this, but hopefully, it would be fine.

It was. When Amyas tilted his head to look at Mordred, Mordred was smiling down at him. He didn't ask Amyas to move away or to stop, so Amyas stayed right where he was, taking a deep breath and enjoying the feeling of someone holding him up.

"I don't want you to rush into anything," Mordred murmured. He squeezed Amyas's hand.

Amyas found himself smiling. "I don't have to rush anymore."

"Exactly."

"And it's thanks to you."

"Not really. I took you along when I left, but you could have done that any time. I was convenient because you managed to find a safe place to spend the first few weeks after leaving the lake, but you're strong, Amyas, much stronger than you think."

"Maybe strength isn't what I needed."

"What do you think you needed, then?"

Amyas bit on his lower lip. "A push forward. To be shown that I would be okay. Support for what I want, even though I don't know what that is."

"Well, you have all of that with me. I don't expect anything from you, not like your parents and Necsa did. Whatever you want to do, you're free to do it."

"Even if it involves leaving you?"

Mordred hesitated, and Amyas held his breath. For now, there was nothing between them, but that could change. Amyas hoped it would.

"Even if you leave," Mordred eventually said. "I can't say

I'll be happy if you do, because I quite like you, but you do what you need to do. We should all do that."

"What do *you* need to do?"

"What I'm already doing. I need to work against the conclave. I need to save the people they hunt and kill."

Amyas wondered if that was what he needed to do, too. He wanted his life to have a meaning that went beyond getting married.

Could this be it?

CHAPTER SEVEN

Amyas laughed and put a bit of bread between his lips, and Mordred couldn't look away.

He never could, and he knew some people had noticed. He could feel Bayard and Eudocia's gazes — and probably at least half the heroes in the dining room tonight — on him and Amyas, but he couldn't find it in himself to be sorry or angry about it.

Except for the fact that Bayard and Eudocia would be gloating because they'd been right and Mordred *was* interested in Amyas.

Who wouldn't be? Amyas was pretty much perfect, at least for Mordred. He was sweet and gentle, but also fierce and strong. He didn't know what he wanted from life, but he didn't let that get him down. He was training with Eudocia every day, and he'd started doing yoga with Mordred.

It was torture.

Mordred hadn't been able to focus since they'd started doing it together. Amyas's body was lithe and soft, but also bendable. Mordred had seen the proof of that as they did yoga, and now, he couldn't stop thinking about it and what Amyas might be like in his bed.

He needed to stop. It was true that Amyas had given him hints that he might be interested in him as much as he was in Amyas, but neither had said anything, and Mordred was afraid to. He didn't want to ruin what he and Amyas had. It felt too fragile and precious.

They could be friends and limit themselves to that. It might be the best thing to do, actually. Amyas still didn't know what he wanted to do with his life, and Mordred didn't want to push him in any way, including being with him. If something happened between them, it might make Amyas decide to stay. It wouldn't be fair to him, not when he didn't know if that was what he wanted.

Could Mordred make that decision for him, though? Amyas had left the village so he would be able to make his own decisions, and Mordred didn't want to take that away from him. He would be doing just that if he decided on his own that they shouldn't be together.

They needed to talk. It would make it easier for everyone. Mordred wasn't sure how to bring it up in a conversation, though.

So he hadn't. Instead, he kept on watching Amyas and admiring him every chance he got. If anything was going to happen between them, neither of them needed to push it. They could go slow and see what happened, and that was what Mordred had decided to do.

Amyas was beautiful, and Mordred was pretty sure no one had missed the way he looked at the undine. It wasn't only Amyas's beauty that was fascinating, though. There was so much more to him than that. He was curious and eager to learn. He wanted to help and explore the world.

Mordred wanted to be there with him every step of the way. He was fascinated, and even though he'd told Eudocia and Bayard he didn't want to think about a relationship, he couldn't help but do just that. What would it be like to be with Amyas? Could they make it work, even though they shared a home with so many people? Other heroes managed, and Mordred wanted to do the same. He couldn't stop thinking about it, no matter how hard he tried.

He wanted Amyas in his life.

An elbow in the ribs made him turn around. He glared at

Bayard, especially since he knew what Bayard wanted. "What?"

"You're staring."

"And?"

"And nothing. I just thought you should know."

Mordred peeked at Amyas, but he was still focused on Dimitri. "I don't know what to do," Mordred confessed.

"I'm not going to tease you and act as if I don't know what you're talking about. Have you talked to him?"

"Not really. It's obvious to both of us are interested, but it's almost like neither of us wants to do anything about it. We're afraid to upset the balance."

"Well, it will have to break if you want something to happen."

Mordred glared. "Don't you think I know that? But this is the first time he's away from the lake and his family. I don't want to clip his wings."

"Who said you would clip his wings? He left the lake and his parents because he wanted to make his own decisions and live his life the way he wants to. That includes whether or not he should be with you. Talk to him. Let him make that decision in the way his parents never allowed him to."

Mordred knew Bay was right. He needed to be brave, just like he'd been when he'd left the conclave. Even if Amyas told him he wasn't ready for anything, that would be okay. As long as Amyas was safe and happy, Mordred would be, too.

When Amyas turned to look at him, Mordred smiled. Amyas's answering smile was beautiful and made Mordred want to reach out to him and grab him, pull him into his lap, and tell him he never wanted to let him go.

He didn't. Instead, he listened to what Amyas had to say and answered accordingly. He finished eating his dinner and allowed himself to sink into the feeling that he was home—with his family.

"You weren't chatty over dinner," Amyas said as Mordred walked him to his room after dinner.

Mordred wasn't sure what to do, and he didn't like it. He was used to making decisions. He was the one who'd gone against the conclave, who protected people, yet in this situation, he was lost. Amyas was much more important to him than any of the people he'd been with in the past decades, and he was terrified of doing something stupid and losing him. "I was thinking," he said.

Amyas nodded. "Do you want to take a walk outside?"

Mordred couldn't help but smile. "I'd be delighted."

"Good. I think I need some time away from the noise. There's always a lot of people here. I didn't expect that."

"Why not?" Mordred asked as he opened the back door and held it so Amyas could slip out. "You knew that a lot of people lived here."

"I did, but I thought all of you would be warriors and nothing else. Instead, you're a family, and all the heroes are here almost every night. It's beautiful to see, but it's also noisy."

"I can't deny that's the truth. You'll get used to it if you stay, though."

Mordred decided to take a risk and held out his hand. Amyas stared for a moment, but he didn't give Mordred the time to start thinking it might have been a bad idea. He took Mordred's hand and squeezed, and when they started walking, they linked their fingers together so they wouldn't have to stop holding hands.

Amyas was silent as they walked, which was strange. He was never silent. He always had something to talk about or questions to ask. It was almost never anything important, but Amyas loved learning, and he was so curious. Mordred was more than happy to answer all his questions, but tonight, there wasn't even one, so much that Mordred was starting to worry. "Is everything okay?" he asked.

Amyas smiled in the darkness, but it was only a shadow of his usual smiles. "Of course."

Mordred needed to put more lamps outside so he would be able to see Amyas better even during the night. "You're quiet. Are you sure everything is okay?"

"I didn't realize you worried about me that much."

Mordred squeezed Amyas's hand. "I do. It took me by surprise, but I'll always worry about you, even if you decide to leave. I just wanted you to know you can come to me for anything. I'll listen to you and try to help as best as I can." That was the only thing Mordred could do, and he hoped Amyas would take advantage of it. If he didn't, well, Mordred would find another way to help the man he was falling in love with.

Amyas didn't know what to say. He might be quiet tonight, but it truly wasn't anything to worry about, even though Mordred seemed to think it was. He was just thinking about what was next for him.

He loved living here. He loved training with Eudocia, doing yoga with Mordred, and feeling like even though he'd arrived only a few weeks ago, he was already part of this family. It was a feeling he'd never had, not even with his own blood family, and he didn't want to lose it.

He also didn't want to lose Mordred.

A lot of people in Amyas's position would have taken advantage of the fact that he was free from his family. He could explore the world and do whatever he wanted, yet here he was, having no intention of ever leaving this house if he had a choice. And now, Mordred was telling him he didn't have to.

Amyas had already known Mordred wouldn't kick him out and that he would keep his promises. That was all Amyas wanted. He'd thought he needed a safe place to think and make decisions, but he'd already decided what he wanted to do with his life, hadn't he? He wanted to help people. He wanted to train and become as good a warrior as Mordred and everyone else in this place. He wanted to do something his parents would never expect him to do.

He realized he was still letting his parents influence him, but he didn't think it mattered. What worried him was the fact that it felt too easy. "I thought it would be harder," he confessed. Mordred had offered to listen to him, and Amyas wasn't going to say no.

"What do you mean?"

"Leaving my family. Building a new life. I thought that even if I ever managed to get away from the lake, I would be on my own. I would have to learn to do things with no one there to support me. Instead, it's the opposite. I have you and everyone else, and as happy as I am about it, I'm also confused because I feel I didn't work for it."

"You don't have to work for anything. I want you here, and I know the others do, too. We like you. You feel like you're part of our family because you are. I can't talk for everyone, but I *can* talk for myself, and I don't want you to leave. You might because you need to learn how to be on your own and things like that, but trust me. It's not necessary. You don't have to learn to be on your own. You don't have to be on your own, period. No one expects you to have to survive alone."

"What do you think about me not having a soul?" That was something else Amyas was starting to worry about.

He'd always felt like he was fine without one, but it had been repeated to him that he needed one and that he wouldn't be complete until he had one. The only way for him to make that happen would be to marry a human, and especially now that he and Mordred were doing whatever they were doing, he didn't want to think about that. Mordred couldn't give him a soul, though. What if he wanted Amyas to have one? What if Amyas truly wasn't complete without one?

"Nothing. What should I think about it?" Mordred asked.

"You have a soul. I don't."

"And? It's just part of who you are. It doesn't change anything. I like you the way you are, Amyas, and having a soul has nothing to do with it."

Amyas found that hard to believe. At home, having a soul was everything. His parents still resented the fact that they'd never been given the opportunity to have one. They'd pushed all their hopes onto Amyas and his sister, which was one of the reasons Amyas felt guilty. He realized he couldn't live the life they wanted, though. He had to make his own choices, which was why he was here.

"Why do you think having a soul will change you?" Mordred asked.

They were still walking, and Amyas was relieved he didn't have to look at Mordred as he answered. He knew Mordred well enough by now to be sure the man wouldn't hold anything he said against him. He truly just wanted Amyas to be happy, which was something Amyas was still trying to come to terms with. Even his own parents hadn't wanted him to be happy. They'd only cared about him having a soul.

"Well, everyone thinks that's where the important part is, isn't it?" he asked.

"Who is everyone?"

Amyas glared at Mordred, but he wasn't sure Mordred could see him. "It's where the goodness of people is. It's the essence of every living being. It's where you can find reason, feelings, all of that. What am I if I don't have a soul? Am I even a human being?" Amyas poured his heart out, and for the first time, he felt lighter.

He'd never been able to have this kind of conversation with his parents. He understood why they wanted him to have a soul. Everything he'd just told Mordred was what they had told him all his life. They wanted their children to have souls. They felt like Amyas and his sister wouldn't be complete if they didn't have one.

Amyas wasn't so sure. Still, even though he didn't think he was making a mistake by refusing a soul, he couldn't help but wonder. Could he ever be complete without one? Or was he a monster? If the soul was where reason and goodness resided, what did the fact that he didn't have one say about him?

Mordred stopped and turned to face him. Amyas was afraid to look at him, but he knew he had to. He wanted to see what Mordred thought about him in Mordred's eyes.

That was where the soul resided, wasn't it? In Mordred's eyes, Amyas could see everything Mordred felt. There was no fear or disgust. There was nothing but affection, and it made Amyas's heart beat faster.

"Do you really believe everything you just said?" Mordred asked.

"I don't know. It's what I've always been told. That's why I'm not sure what I'm doing. If I could have a soul without getting married to someone I don't love, I would take it. As it is, though, I can't because I can't find it in myself to do that. I feel it would cheapen the soul, and that's not what I want."

"I don't think you need a soul," Mordred said gently. "If you want one, I'm sure we can find a way to make it happen. But I doubt it would change who you are. You're perfect even without a soul, Amyas. After all, no one knows what a soul is or even if it actually exists."

Amyas snorted. "My parents would beg to differ."

"I don't care what your parents would do. I told you. If you want a soul, I'll make it happen. If you don't care about that, though, I don't see a reason to freak out. I like you just the way you are. I got to know you without a soul, and you seem perfect to me. If it's something you want to explore, we can, but I don't think you need it."

Amyas didn't want to think anymore. Mordred was giving him everything he'd ever wanted and had never hoped he would get.

Amyas threw his arms around Mordred's neck. Mordred made a strange sound that sounded like a squeak, but when Amyas kissed him, he didn't push him away.

Instead, he kissed Amyas back.

It was perfection. Amyas had imagined this moment several times, but his imagination paled in front of how it was. Mordred cradled Amyas into his arms, kissing him as if he were the only thing that mattered. He kissed Amyas until Amyas was out of breath, but neither of them stopped.

This was a decision Amyas was making, and he wouldn't regret it. Whatever happened in the future, whatever happened with Mordred, Amyas would always have this.

He would always have the capacity to make decisions, which was why he'd left his village.

"Are you sure this is what you want?" Mordred asked, his voice barely more than a whisper.

"I've never been more sure of anything. Take me to your room, Mordred."

Mordred didn't ask if Amyas was sure again. Instead, he gathered Amyas into his arms—which wasn't hard considering how much bigger Mordred was—and carried him to the house. Amyas buried his face against Mordred's neck. He wasn't ashamed of what was happening, but he didn't want to make a spectacle of themselves, and there was no way anyone would misunderstand if they saw Mordred and Amyas walk in.

Luckily for them, everyone seemed to be busy elsewhere. Amyas knew where Mordred's bedroom was, even though he'd never been in it, and his heart raced as they reached the door. Mordred didn't even have to put Amyas down to open it. Amyas had never been particularly turned on by men stronger than he was, but seeing how easily Mordred could manhandle him gave him a thrill.

Mordred kicked the door closed behind them, but instead of throwing Amyas onto the bed as Amyas had hoped he would, he hovered there, clearly not sure what to do.

That wasn't a problem because Amyas could take things into his own hands. The fact that he could, that Mordred was letting him, made him happy.

Amyas pushed himself closer and kissed Mordred again. That seemed to trigger Mordred to move again, and he stepped toward the bed. He was gentle as he lowered Amyas onto the mattress. It was almost as if Amyas was precious to him, and the thought made Amyas feel warm inside—and tight in his pants.

Mordred pressed himself against Amyas, and Amyas decided to focus on him.

Everything else could wait.

He hooked his arms around Mordred's neck once again, pulling him even closer. For some reason, it made Mordred chuckle. Instead of coming back like Amyas wanted to, he propped himself up on both his elbows and looked down at Amyas. "What did you have in mind?" he asked.

"That it's not the right moment to talk. I just want to feel you."

"And you will. I don't want to do something you're not ready for, though."

Amyas would have rolled his eyes if it hadn't been obvious that Mordred truly cared. "You're not my first boyfriend."

"That's good to hear. I still want you to tell me what you expect from me."

Amyas grinned. He felt freer than he had in a long time, maybe ever. It was all thanks to Mordred, and he couldn't wait for what was next, whatever it was. "Whatever feels good."

Mordred huffed. "That doesn't tell me anything. Come on, Amyas. Don't make this hard for me."

Amyas thrust his hips upward. "It doesn't feel like I have to make things harder."

Mordred groaned. "That was bad."

"Then maybe you should shut me up."

Mordred arched a brow. "Should I? What do you want me to shut you up with?"

Amyas grinned and kissed Mordred again. This time, though, he didn't limit himself to that. He also wrapped an arm around Mordred, cupping Mordred's ass and squeezing. Mordred made a strange sound, almost a squeak again, and Amyas moved back. "Too much?" he asked.

Mordred shook his head and kissed him again. "Not enough," he murmured.

Since Mordred seemed to be okay with this, Amyas pushed a hand inside the back of Mordred's jeans. It was a tight fit, but he wouldn't change it for anything, since the jeans made Mordred's ass look incredible. Amyas squeezed, smiling at the feeling of supple flesh under his fingertips. He bit his lower lip as Mordred kissed down his neck. Maybe they should have talked. He wasn't sure what Mordred wanted or didn't want, although knowing Mordred, he wouldn't be offended if Amyas did something he wasn't up for. He would just tell Amyas to stop.

That, more than anything, pushed Amyas to do what he wanted.

He slipped his fingertips between Mordred's ass cheeks and held his breath. He expected Mordred to push him away, but instead, Mordred wiggled. Amyas's eyebrows shot up his forehead. "I didn't expect you to like this," he murmured.

Mordred gently bit Amyas his neck. "I'm pretty sure I would like anything if it comes from you."

"I suppose we'll see." Amyas didn't want to push his luck, though, so instead of doing what he wanted, he sucked in his stomach, moved his hands to the front of both their pants, and swiftly unfastened them. Mordred seemed amused, but thankfully, he helped Amyas, raising his hips to give him more space. He never stopped kissing down Amyas's neck, which made it difficult to focus.

Once Amyas had both their pants undone, he pushed Mordred's down his hips. Mordred helped again, moving back just enough that he could push his jeans lower. It wasn't going fast enough for Amyas's taste, so he decided to leave Mordred to it and pushed down his own pants. Thankfully, he didn't wear jeans, and the soft cotton was easy to get rid of. He kicked it down, eager to feel Mordred's flesh against his.

When it finally happened, it was like heaven.

Amyas groaned and threw his head back. He wanted so much more, but he was almost afraid to ask. Luckily, that didn't seem to stop Mordred, who pushed Amyas's shirt up to his armpits. It got stuck there, but that seemed to be okay with Mordred, who kissed down Amyas's chest, stopping at his nipple. He gave it a lick, then a bite. Amyas hadn't expected that, and he squeaked, trying to push himself into a sitting position.

Mordred wasn't having any of that, though. "You don't like it?" he asked. His voice was rough, and it made Amyas feel warm.

"I love it. I was just surprised."

"I can continue, then?"

"Are you kidding? You have to continue." Amyas was ready to beg, if that was what it took.

Luckily, it wasn't. He didn't even need to ask twice before Mordred went back to his nipples. Mordred expanded his exploration to the rest of Amyas's chest, and Amyas could do nothing but lay there and take everything Mordred wanted to give him.

It was heaven.

"I want you to know I care," Mordred said against Amyas's skin. "That you are important to me and everyone else in this house. I want to give you everything you want."

Amyas swallowed. He couldn't answer, not when his throat felt tight. He believed everything Mordred was telling him, and he was grateful.

More importantly, he was horny.

He smiled and pulled Mordred up. "What I want right now is you. It's more than enough, but you have to give it to me."

"Always."

Dammit. Why was Mordred so perfect? Amyas kissed him again, his hands roaming over both their bodies. He was trying to finish stripping them as he kissed Mordred, but it was hard when they couldn't seem to put more than a few inches between each other. Amyas was tempted to tear them off, but he didn't have a lot of clothes, and he'd rather keep these intact.

Eventually, they managed to get rid of their clothes. Amyas didn't know how they did it, but he didn't care. The only thing he cared about was Mordred's naked body on top of his. He wanted so many different things that it was hard for him to choose one. He wanted to come. He wanted to watch Mordred come. He wanted Mordred inside him, and he wanted to be inside Mordred.

He wanted everything.

It was overwhelming, and he was relieved when Mordred, just like always, took charge. He took care of Amyas, making him feel cherished, but also like he had a choice. It wasn't every move Mordred made. If Amyas had a problem with it, he just had to say it, and Mordred would stop.

Instead of pressing his body on top of Amyas's, Mordred moved down. Amyas couldn't look away as Mordred kissed his stomach, his hipbones, his bellybutton. Then he went even lower, breathing hot against Amyas's cock.

Amyas swallowed, and so did Mordred. He wrapped his lips around the head of Amyas's cock, and they were warm and slick and the best thing Amyas had ever experienced. He let his head drop against the pillow and screwed his eyes shut for a moment, but he wanted to watch. He hoped he and Mordred would do this again and again, but just in case, he wanted this moment to be seared into his brain.

Mordred was beautiful, and it didn't have anything to do with the fact that he was sucking Amyas's cock. Amyas knew Mordred would protest if he told him, so he wouldn't, but he still thought it. Mordred had a raw kind of beauty, something powerful that made Amyas feel safe. His piercings glinted in the soft light that came from outside, and while Amyas wished he could see more, this kind of light made everything softer, including Mordred and what they were doing.

Amyas reached out, opening his arms. "Come here," he murmured.

Mordred let go of Amyas's cock. "Already?"

"Yes. I need you here."

Mordred sat on his knees and hesitated as he looked at the nightstand. "Should I grab the lube?"

"Not today." This didn't feel like that kind of evening anymore. It felt deeper, and Amyas just wanted to feel Mordred move against him. There was still passion between them, but it was softer and gentler, and Amyas wanted more.

He always wanted more with Mordred, and he suspected that wasn't going to change anytime soon.

Mordred moved up, spreading himself over Amyas. Amyas wrapped himself around him, smiling at the weight and the feeling of being anchored. He pressed his nose and lips against Mordred's neck, smiling at his smell. He was warm and perfect, especially when he started moving. His cock felt heavy against Amyas's groin, but also perfect, and Amyas knew he'd made the right choice. This was the way to make love tonight, gentle and soft and loving.

And it was all those things. They moved together, their bodies fitting like they were meant to be one. The smells and sensations were overwhelming, and this time, Amyas kept his eyes shut. He had to, because they prickled with tears that he couldn't explain.

A few rolled down his cheeks when he came, hiding his face against Mordred's neck and crying out in pleasure and happiness, and so many other emotions that it felt like his chest was about to burst. Amyas lost himself in the moment, and when he felt Mordred come against him, he smiled.

This was what Amyas had always wanted — the opportunity to make his own choices, to be with Mordred because he wanted to and not because his parents did. He was never giving this up, not if he had a choice.

And for the first time, he did.

CHAPTER EIGHT

Mordred couldn't stop smiling. He'd been this way since Amyas had arrived at the house, but now even more so.

Mordred and Amyas hadn't talked about what their nights together meant, but Mordred didn't think they had to. Everyone knew they were together, and everyone was happy for them.

Mordred had never felt happier.

He'd thought he could do without this—without Amyas—but it had been stupid. He couldn't do without Amyas, not even if he wanted to, and he didn't.

He had Amyas in his life, and he couldn't wait to see what happened next. He could see them being together in the long term. Amyas was working to become a fighter, and he wanted to help the heroes. Mordred's first instinct was to say no because it was dangerous, but he couldn't do that to Amyas.

Amyas was finally finding his footing in life. He was making his own decisions, and he was obviously happy. Mordred's protective side was going to have to take the back seat and let Amyas do whatever he wanted with his life. That was the only way Amyas would be happy, and his happiness was everything Mordred wanted, even though he hadn't seen it coming.

"You haven't stopped smiling," Bayard grumbled.

Mordred grinned at him. "So? I thought that was what you wanted."

"I didn't think it would be so annoying."

Mordred felt the absurd urge to stick his tongue out, but he didn't. "I don't get it. You and Eudocia were on my case because you wanted me and Amyas to be together, and now that we are, you're grumpy."

Bayard waved Mordred's words away. "It's because I'm jealous, okay? I'm happy for you and Amyas, and I wish you the best. I also wish I had someone who makes me smile the way Amyas makes you smile, though."

That made Mordred frown. "Didn't you have a boyfriend?"

"We broke up ages ago. You don't have to worry about it. It was amicable, so you won't have trouble in the house."

Bayard's answer made Mordred frown even harder. Was that really what his friend thought about him? That he was only worried about the house, the heroes, and the mission, and that he didn't care about his friends' happiness? "You know you can talk to me about anything, right?"

Bayard arched a brow. "Really, boss?"

"I'm not your boss," Mordred protested.

"You are."

"I'm not *just* your boss, then. I'm your friend, or at least, I hope I am."

Bayard's expression softened. "You're one of my best friends, and I don't want you to worry. I'm fine, even though I'm grumpy."

"And jealous," Mordred pointed out.

"And jealous," Bayard conceded. "It won't last forever, though. Eventually, I'm sure I'll find someone, too. Besides, happiness shouldn't have anything to do with someone else. I'm the one making my own happiness, right?"

"Right," Mordred agreed. Secretly, though, he thought that Amyas had a lot to do with *his* happiness.

Mordred had been content before. He loved his job, loved taking care of people, and protecting them, and he was still doing that. He also loved his friends, and they were an indispensable part of his life.

Amyas was different. He made Mordred smile like no one else could. He made Mordred see that he wasn't dead inside like he'd thought he was and that he deserved to be happy.

For so long, Mordred had believed that his only goal in life should be to protect the people he'd been killing only a few hundred years ago. If he wasn't focused on that, he wasn't doing a good job like he needed to. He knew that was wrong now. He was still focused on his mission, but he understood it couldn't be his entire life. He had to find the balance he hadn't since he'd started it, and it was harder than he'd expected.

That didn't mean he wasn't happy, though. Amyas made him the happiest person on earth, and he never wanted it to stop. He also wanted his best friend to find someone, but he didn't know how to help, or even if he could. This was something Bayard would have to fix on his own, no matter how much Mordred wished he could help.

"Enough talking about your love life, though," Bayard said, straightening in his chair. "We're here to talk about the conclave."

And they did, for an hour. There was nothing new, no matter how hard they tried. Mordred was worried. It wasn't like the conclave to stay silent for so long, and he suspected they were planning something. What that something might be was a mystery, and he didn't like mysteries. They never ended well for anyone.

He was relieved when someone knocked on his office door. "Come in," he called out, his smile widening when he saw it was Amyas. Bayard grumbled something and got to his feet.

Amyas shook his head. "Sit down. I brought both of you lunch."

"You didn't have to," Mordred said. When Amyas was close enough, he snatched him by the waist and pulled him closer, kissing him on the lips.

Bayard groaned, but when Mordred looked at him, he was smiling. "I'm going to go," Bayard said, but he should have known better.

Amyas glared at him and pointed at the chair he'd gotten up from. "Sit down. You don't have to go. I brought enough food for both of you, and I'm going to make sure you eat it."

"You realize you're not my father, right?" Bayard asked, but he sat down anyway.

"I'm much too young and pretty to be your father," Amyas answered.

While Bayard was spluttering, Amyas stepped outside of the office and grabbed a tray from one of the tables in the hall-way. Mordred's stomach growled when he saw the food on it, and when Amyas came closer again to give him his plate, he grabbed his hand and kissed the palm. "Thank you," he murmured.

Amyas smiled. "Someone has to make sure the two of you eat and don't just focus on work. I'll be back to grab the plates in half an hour. I want to find them empty."

Bayard was still grumbling, but Mordred suspected he was as touched by the gesture as Mordred.

Amyas didn't have to do this. He didn't have to take care of them or anyone else in the house, yet he was. Mordred sus-pected it was because he needed to feel useful. He was train-ing to help on missions, but it was going to take some time for him to be ready. In the meantime, he seemed to have taken it upon himself to make sure everyone ate and had everything they needed, including Mordred and Bayard.

After one last kiss, Amyas left the office. Mordred grabbed his sandwich and took a bite, but he could feel Bayard's gaze on him. He looked up at him and arched a brow without ask-ing what was wrong—he couldn't with his mouth full.

Bayard chuckled. "You're serious about him, aren't you?"

he asked.

Mordred swallowed. "Why? Did you think I wasn't?"

"I don't know what to think. I knew he was different from your other relationships, but now that I see you together, it's even more obvious. I didn't expect it. You always kept yourself apart, and now, you don't anymore."

Mordred leaned back in his chair. "It's thanks to Amyas. I was so focused on what I thought I was supposed to do that I didn't allow anything else in my life. I thought I didn't deserve love."

"You, out of everyone, deserve love. You've been doing this for two hundred years. You're still blaming yourself for working for the conclave, though."

Mordred sighed. "It was wrong."

"We all were. You can't keep on blaming yourself, though. You've more than atoned for everything you did."

Mordred wasn't convinced Bayard was right, but for the first time in hundreds of years, he hoped he was.

Amyas was mothering everyone. So far, none of the heroes had told him to stop, but he suspected that eventually they would. No one wanted to be mothered by someone who wasn't their mother.

Amyas had always loved taking care of people, though, and doing it in this situation made him feel useful. It also made him feel like he was settling in the house, both with Mordred and with everyone else. He needed to do something, and this was perfect. It left him time to train. It was going to be some time before he was able to go on a mission. Mordred wouldn't allow him to go until he was sure Amyas could defend himself, and Amyas agreed. He had a new life now, and he didn't want to lose it by acting like an idiot.

Still, he should probably talk to Mordred and everyone

else, ask them if what he was doing was okay. A lot of the heroes didn't take care of themselves the way they should. They brushed off their injuries, barely ate, and spent most of their time training. Amyas felt like most of them were trying to atone the same way Mordred was, and while he understood, he didn't think that putting themselves in danger and almost getting killed at least once a week was doing much.

He wanted to do more, which was why he'd organized a movie night.

He had no idea what he was doing or if anyone would come. He hadn't even known movies were a thing until Dimitri had introduced him to them, and he loved them. Dimitri had also said it was something people did together as a family, and that was perfect for what Amyas wanted.

He felt both free and like he belonged to a family at the same time, which was perfection as far as he was concerned. He wanted everything to be even more perfect, and in his eyes, that meant making sure the heroes took care of themselves and *knew* they were family and would always have someone to come back to.

Amyas looked around the living room, his hands on his hips. He'd gotten popcorn, just like Dimitri had said, and he'd put it in big bowls and scattered them around the room. He'd also gathered blankets and pillows so everyone would be comfortable. The living room was big, and there were several couches and armchairs, but he wasn't sure everyone would fit. This way, even those who had to sit on the floor would be comfortable. Besides, the carpet was thick, so they should be okay.

"What are you up to?" someone asked behind Amyas, making him jump.

He turned around and glared at Bayard. "I need to put a bell on you and everyone else in this house. Why are all of you so quiet?"

Bayard shrugged. "Because not being quiet could mean death if we're on a mission. What are you doing?" Bayard peeked around Amyas, his eyes widening when he saw the living room. "What happened here?"

"*I* happened," Amyas explained. "We're having movie night, and before you try getting out of it, you're participating, too."

Bayard groaned. "What if I don't want to? What if I hate movies?"

"Sometimes, we all have to do things we hate." Amyas kissed Bayard's cheek. "I'm sure you'll have fun. Give me a chance, okay?"

Bayard blinked in what looked like surprise. He probably hadn't expected the kiss, and to be honest, Amyas hadn't thought much about it before doing it. It felt right, though. Bayard was one of Mordred's best friends, and Mordred and Amyas were together. All the heroes here were family, but Bayard and Eudocia especially so. The same went for Dimitri. He was Amyas's best friend, and it had nothing to do with the fact that they were the only two supernatural beings in the house.

Amyas was surprised at how many people he had in his life and how much he cared about them already. With Dimitri, he could talk about things no one else—not even Mordred—would understand. Haven still made Amyas nervous, but that was mostly because of how intense he was. It was obvious he cared about Dimitri very much, though, which made him okay in Amyas's book.

Hopefully, this would be an evening in which they all would be able to relax and spend time together.

"I don't know what the others are going to think about this," Bayard said.

Amyas crossed his arms over his chest. "Do I look like I care? Mordred is going to order them to be here, and they'll obey."

Bayard laughed. "You're probably right. Mordred would do pretty much anything you ask him to do, including this."

Amyas was getting worried, though. "You think people will try to get out of it? I don't want to force anyone to spend time with me. It was just a thought."

Bayard's expression softened, and to Amyas's surprise, he reached out and squeezed Amyas's shoulder. "It'll be fine. A few will grumble, but they'll come, and they'll have fun."

Amyas arched a brow. "Does that include you?"

Bayard laughed again. "It does. Don't worry about me. I was just having this conversation with Mordred before you came in to bring us lunch earlier today. I'm happy for both of you, but I'm jealous. I want a cute boyfriend, too."

Amyas blinked. "There are plenty of cute guys here."

"I know, and trust me, I dated my share of them. It's never worked, not in the long term. That's fine. I don't want you to feel like you have to walk on eggshells around me. Like I told Mordred, it'll pass. You just focus on him and on being happy. I'll take care of myself."

Amyas slowly nodded, but he couldn't stop thinking about Bayard's words. Bayard was immortal, just like Mordred and everyone else in the house. It had to be lonely to spend so much time on his own. It wasn't a surprise that he was jealous, but Amyas wished he could do something for him. He didn't know anyone he could introduce to Bayard, though.

"What are we watching, then?" Bayard asked, distracting Amyas.

"I selected a few movies, and I thought we could vote when everyone is here. That way, it will be a family decision."

Bayard stared at Amyas for a moment. "This family thing is important to you, isn't it?" he eventually asked.

"Family is everything."

"Yet you left yours."

"I don't think they truly were my family, not in the sense I mean. They're my parents, but the only thing they care about is me finding a human to marry and leaving the lake. They care about me, but not enough to want me to be happy doing what I want to do."

"I see. Well, I'm happy you found what you were looking for with us. You're a good fit in this family, and you're making it better."

Amyas looked around again. He wasn't sure about that, but he sure was going to try. He wanted these heroes to be happy and to see that their lives didn't have to be confined to training and saving supernatural beings. They'd made big mistakes in the past, but they'd realized that, and they were working hard to change things. That, to Amyas, meant everything.

Mordred blinked when he walked into the living room after dinner. He'd noticed that everyone in the house was buzzing with expectation and excitement, but he hadn't given it much thought, focused as he was on what the conclave was plotting. He had no idea what was going on, but he hadn't expected *this*.

"What's going on?" he asked.

Amyas, who was standing by talking to Dimitri, turned toward him, beaming. "I didn't expect all of them to be here."

Mordred hooked an arm around Amyas's waist and pulled him closer. "What did you do?"

Amyas's cheeks flushed, but he didn't look away. "I probably should have asked first, but I thought having a family movie night would be fun."

So that was what was happening. Mordred looked around again, and sure enough, Amyas had thought of everything. There was popcorn in bowls scattered around the room, blankets and pillows, bottles of water and soda, and the TV was already on. A few heroes were looking around, looking lost, but most had already settled onto the couches or the floor, and they were talking with each other and obviously having fun.

Mordred's chest felt tight with emotion. Before Amyas had entered his life, he hadn't realized the heroes who worked with him were his family. When he'd recruited them, he hadn't meant for it to happen. He needed help working against the conclave, and who better to do that than heroes who had seen the light? But living together had pushed them closer, and Amyas was right—they *were* a family. It was a huge, noisy one, but it was perfect. No matter how alone Mordred had felt in the past decades, he never truly had been.

"Is it okay?" Amyas asked.

Mordred couldn't speak for a moment, and he answered by kissing the top of Amyas's head. He had to lean down because Amyas was so much shorter, but it didn't matter. "It's perfect," he finally murmured.

"Are you sure? I wanted everyone to do something together, and I couldn't think of anything else, not without leaving the house. Dimitri mentioned other things we could do, but this was the simplest."

"It's perfect," Mordred repeated. He doubted Amyas would believe him. He was insecure, which made sense when all his family had told him since he was old enough to hear it was that he would only be worth something when he got a soul. "I should have thought about doing something like this sooner, but obviously, I needed you to do it."

"I don't understand," Amyas murmured.

Mordred pulled him to the side. They were still in the living room, but they were close to the door, and they had some privacy. He kissed Amyas's nose and smiled at him. "Before you got here, the only thing we focused on was work. We still do that, but your presence has made us feel more human. It has made *me* realize that I needed to stop punishing myself." Even though it was hard.

More often than not, Mordred's first thought was that he needed to be doing more, that he had to stop focusing on his private life and work harder. It was wrong, though. Living just for work wasn't living, and that thought put the few times when Mordred had almost been killed while on a mission into perspective. He hadn't had anyone to come back to, and he'd been reckless.

He wouldn't do that anymore, and he suspected he wasn't the only one when he looked around once again. The others didn't have Amyas in their life the way he did, but Amyas was still a loving presence to them, and he was making everyone know how much he cared about them. Mordred suspected it would make a huge difference in the way they behaved, both on missions and at home.

"I'm surprised you managed to get almost everyone to come."

Amyas nodded. "It wasn't easy. A few couldn't get out of their plans, but they promised to be here next time."

"There's going to be a next time, then?"

"I hope so. I like this. I like seeing all the heroes gathered here, relaxed, and having fun. Usually, you're all gloomy and obsessed with work. This is a nice change."

A change that happened thanks to Amyas.

Mordred kissed him again, on the lips this time. "Thank you."

"What are you thanking me for? I didn't do anything."

"That's where you're wrong. You're doing a lot, and you don't even realize it. You're bringing us together as more than a group of colleagues. With your addition, we truly are a family."

Amyas looked like he didn't know what to say, so instead

of waiting for him to answer, Mordred took his hand and pulled him toward one of the couches. It had been left empty, probably for him and Amyas.

Bayard was sitting on the floor next to the couch. He nodded at Mordred when Mordred sat down, pulling Amyas with him. Eudocia was there, too, leaning against her boyfriend. Their heads were close together and they were both smiling, and Mordred couldn't remember the last time he'd seen her so relaxed.

Mordred and the others had always been more focused on the job and keeping everyone safe than on their personal lives. Things had changed, and it was for the better, even though Mordred wouldn't have thought so a few months ago.

He wrapped his arm around Amyas's shoulder, and Amyas grabbed the remote control from the coffee table. "We have to choose a movie," he declared. They were a few groans, but most heroes sat up straighter. "I preselected a few. Keep in mind that I've never watched any of these."

He said a few titles, and the groans in the room turned louder. There were also a few cheers, and everyone started pitching in.

Mordred didn't care what movie they watched as long as he could watch it like this, with Amyas in his arms and his family around him. He could see them doing this for years to come — hopefully, decades. Everyone in the room was immortal, and that meant they had an infinite time to love each other and be a family. Mordred would never have realized that without Amyas, and he was more than ever grateful to the conclave for deciding to send two heroes to the lake. Without that, Mordred wouldn't have met Amyas, and his life would be so much emptier.

CHAPTER NINE

The evening had been great. There had been a few grumbles at the choice of the movie, but everyone had gone along with it, and they'd had fun, or at least, Amyas hoped so. No one had complained, not even Mordred, so Amyas took that as a win.

"When do you think we could do this again?" he asked as he and Mordred walked toward Mordred's room.

Amyas still had his own bedroom, but he hadn't spent the night there since he and Mordred had gotten together. He wasn't planning on doing so, either. He was perfectly fine spending every single evening in Mordred's bed, and he hoped that wouldn't change anytime soon.

"Maybe you can make it a weekly thing. I had fun, and I don't think I was the only one."

Amyas's heart felt like it was about to burst. He'd been afraid of everyone's reaction when he'd come up with the idea, but it had been good. Even the people who hadn't managed to come that night had promised they would be there the next time, and Amyas was looking forward to it. He had thousands of movies to catch up on and an eternal life to do it.

"I'll send an email to everyone to let them know it's happening," Mordred continued. "You pick a day, and everyone who can be there will be."

Amyas frowned. "You're not going to force them to come, are you?"

For some reason, that made Mordred smile. "Would I do

something like that?"

"For me, you definitely would."

Mordred laughed. "You're not wrong. I would do pretty much anything for you."

The words still surprised Amyas. Mordred wasn't lying, but after feeling like his parents cared about only one aspect of Amyas, it was a big change. More than ever, Amyas was convinced he'd done the right thing by asking Mordred to take him along when he'd left the lake.

Amyas felt better than he ever had. He was happier, too, and he looked forward to what the next days, weeks, and months would bring. He knew that eventually, something would change. They might lose a hero, although it was tough to kill heroes. Some would be wounded, and Amyas and everyone else would be worried. This would never fade, though. They would always have each other, and they would always be a family.

"Are you tired?" Mordred asked.

They'd reached his bedroom door, and he opened it to let Amyas pass.

Amyas smiled as he walked in front of Mordred. "What do you think?"

Mordred laughed again. "That it was a stupid question."

"You're not wrong. It *was* kind of stupid. Do you really think I could be tired with you in my bed?"

"Do I have to remind you that this is *my* bed and not yours?"

Amyas rolled his eyes. "You don't. I feel like it's our bed now."

"You're not wrong. Maybe you should just move in here with me."

Amyas grinned. He hadn't expected the offer, but he wasn't surprised it had come. "We can do it tomorrow. Tonight, I have plans."

Mordred closed the bedroom door behind himself. "Oh? Am I part of these plans?"

"You definitely are."

This was fun. When Amyas had thought about his future and the relationship he would have with his human spouse, he hadn't thought it would be like this. He'd expected it to be stilted and for his spouse to eventually cheat on him. That was one of the reasons he'd always refused to find a human to marry. Why should he do that when he already knew what would happen if he did?

But Mordred was different, and Amyas was more than ready to marry him if he ever asked. Amyas doubted it would happen, though. They didn't need to be married, not when it wouldn't give Amyas a soul. It wouldn't change anything in their relationship, so they might as well continue like this. Besides, they'd only just met. It was way too soon for either of them to think about marriage.

Mordred wouldn't hold it against Amyas if he refused to go that way. He'd understand, because he knew Amyas's back story with marriage. He was the perfect man, and once again, Amyas found himself grateful for how things had gone. It could easily have been a disaster, but he'd trusted the right person, and he would never regret it.

He took off his sweater and dropped it onto the chair by the bathroom door. "I had fun," he said.

"I think everyone had fun," Mordred answered. He sounded amused.

"I'm tempted to put on one of the movies everyone groaned about next time."

"Please do. It will be fun to watch them bitch about it."

Amyas frowned. "I don't want the others to dislike me because of it, though."

"I don't think anyone could dislike you, for whatever reason. You're pretty much perfect."

Amyas sat on the edge of the mattress and shook his head. "I'm not perfect. No one is, not even you."

"I'm going to sound incredibly corny, but I think that you're perfect for *me*. You certainly feel like you are."

It *was* corny, but it made Amyas's cheeks feel warm, and he couldn't help but smile. He'd never felt perfect. His parents had always made sure to let him know that he wasn't and that he needed a soul to become complete. Amyas had believed them, but Mordred was making him see they'd been wrong. He was convinced Amyas was perfect the way he was, and Amyas was starting to believe him.

"Did I scare you?" Mordred asked.

Amyas shook his head. "No. I don't think you could ever scare me."

Mordred crouched in front of Amyas and gently took his hand. "I feel this turned serious quickly. What did you say about those plans for the night?"

Amyas grinned. He was more than ready to forget about all of this and focus on Mordred.

Mordred knew what Amyas had planned just by the way he smiled, and his cock twitched in his jeans as both of them got to their feet and faced each other.

"You said you wouldn't mind . . . being on the receiving end of things," Amyas said.

The conversation wasn't going where Mordred had expected it. "I don't. I can't say it's something I often do, but that has more to do with the fact that I don't often date."

Amyas leaned closer. "Is it something you'd want to do with me?"

Amyas didn't know there was little Mordred *didn't* want to do with him. "If you want it, too."

Amyas arched a brow. "I wouldn't have asked if I didn't."

He reached for Mordred's jeans.

Mordred let him do what he wanted, which apparently was open his pants and push them down his legs. Mordred moved to help him, but Amyas grabbed his legs and shook his head.

"Let me," he said.

Mordred froze. He wasn't used to people taking care of him. He was the one who took care of everyone here, from heroes who left the conclave to the supernatural beings and humans they helped. Mordred was in charge and everyone looked up to him, even Eudocia and Bayard, who were his seconds. Even Amyas did it, although their relationship had shifted now that they were sleeping together.

"I know you're not used to this," Amyas continued as he unlaced Mordred's boots and took them off, then focused on his socks. "But I want to take care of you the way you've been taking care of me. I want to show you I can."

"I already know you can." Mordred reached out and gently stroked Amyas's hair. "You're one of the strongest people I know. Needing someone sometimes doesn't make you weak."

"The same goes for you," Amyas said as he straightened and hooked his fingers at the bottom of Mordred's sweater and pulled it up and off Mordred's body. "Needing me or anyone else to take care of you sometimes doesn't make you weak. It makes you human, and I like you that way. I don't want whatever we're doing to be one-sided and for you to have to rescue me and take care of me."

"I do it because I want to," Mordred said. The cool air of the bedroom felt good on his overheated skin.

Amyas kissed Mordred's nipple and smiled up at him. "I know. And I'm doing this because I want to." He dropped to his knees, kissed both of Mordred's inner thighs, and looked up at him. "I don't think I'll ever forget the first time we were together. You took care of me this way, but you also stopped when I asked you to. I'll do the same tonight, although I hope you won't ask me to stop. I want to do this for you, but also for me."

There was no way Mordred would tell Amyas to stop. Well, maybe he would if Amyas brought up whips and chains, but that was because Mordred was boring. He liked his sex passionate but gentle, and with nothing but him and Amyas in bed.

He forgot all about whips when Amyas licked the head of his cock. He wondered if this was how Amyas had felt that first night when Mordred had sucked him off. He'd been watching, and Mordred was doing the same now. He couldn't look away, not when Amyas wrapped his lips around his cock, or when he reached down to undo his own pants. The fact that his fingers came back from doing that holding a packet of lube almost made Mordred laugh, but Amyas did something with his tongue at the same time, so instead, he groaned.

Mordred dug his fingertips into Amyas's hair. He was going to have to feel anchored for what came next. He couldn't think of anyone better than Amyas to do this with—he trusted Amyas with everything, especially his body and his heart—but it had been a while, and the last time he'd done this, it hadn't ended too well. The guy he'd been with had been in too much of a rush, and it had hurt.

Amyas wasn't in a rush, though, or if he was, he hid it well. He let go of Mordred's cock for a moment so he could tear open the packet of lube with his teeth, and as he did so, Mordred wrapped his fingers around his cock and jacked himself off a few times. The sight of Amyas on his knees in front of him and how slick his cock was already enthralled him. A lot had to do with Amyas's saliva, but Mordred wanted Amyas all the time, and tonight wasn't any different.

Amyas grinned when he got the packet open and spread the lube on his fingers. He reached behind Mordred, and Mordred held his breath, expecting pain even though he knew it was ridiculous. Amyas frowned for a moment before sucking Mordred's cock into his mouth again. That, coupled with the feeling of his probing and rubbing against Mordred's hole, made Mordred open his legs wider to give him better access. This was Amyas. He wasn't going to hurt Mordred, and Mordred had to focus on that.

It was easy once Amyas threw himself into prepping Mordred. He was enthusiastic both with his mouth and fingers, and even though the stretch was on the edge of becoming painful a few times, Amyas distracted Mordred until Mordred's knees felt like they couldn't hold him up anymore. He reached out for the wall, but he missed it and almost toppled onto the floor, which wrenched Amyas's mouth from Mordred's cock.

"I think you should lay down," Amyas said. He sounded amused but also tense.

Mordred was pretty sure it was because he was about to come and resisting the need, just like Mordred. "I agree," he murmured. He sounded drunk, and he felt that way a bit, too, even though he hadn't had any alcohol tonight.

He turned toward the bed and crawled onto it, lowering himself to his elbows and exposing his ass. He waited for Amyas to do something, and when he didn't, Mordred twisted around to look at him without moving from his position.

The way Amyas was staring at Mordred's ass lit a fire in Mordred's gut. He swallowed a few times before he could speak. "Well?" he asked.

Amyas jerked. "Sorry. I wish we could do it like this, but the difference in height would make kissing uncomfortable, if not impossible."

Mordred hadn't thought of that, but now that he was into this, he wanted a good, hard, and loving fucking, and they could do that without kissing. "You can kiss me all you want later. I'm not going anywhere."

Amyas's gaze turned almost feral. "You're not." He climbed onto the mattress, his cock bobbing between his legs. He cupped both of Mordred's ass cheeks and squeezed them together, then apart.

Mordred shuddered. He needed more, but he was afraid to ask for it, so he stayed silent and let Amyas do whatever he wanted. Amyas being Amyas, he surprised Mordred once again when instead of pushing into him, he licked a stripe from Mordred's balls to his hole.

"Fucking hell," Mordred muttered. He had to hold himself up, or he'd collapse.

Amyas didn't seem to notice as he focused on Mordred's ass. Mordred couldn't have said if this was Amyas's first time rimming someone, mostly because he felt like he couldn't think. He could only feel—cherished, protected, like Amyas made everything good in his word. He'd wanted Amyas to feel this way when it came to him, but he hadn't expected to feel the same way when it came to Amyas.

Mordred lost himself in the moment. He whimpered and shamelessly pushed back against Amyas's tongue and fingers as Amyas did his best to drive him crazy. He felt like he was when he got to the brink of coming, and instead of letting him, Amyas leaned back.

"Why?" Mordred whined.

Amyas didn't answer, not with words. Instead, Mordred felt something warm and hard press against his hole, and he eagerly pressed back against it. He *needed* to be fucked.

Amyas slid inside Mordred as if he belonged there. There was no hint of pain or anything like that, just pleasure and love. Amyas's long hair brushed against Mordred's naked back as he moved inside Mordred, and now Mordred understood why Amyas hadn't wanted to do it like this. He wanted Amyas to surround him and hold him through it, but he couldn't.

It was fine anyway. Mordred felt just as cherished because Amyas took care of him, reaching around him and grabbing his cock, jacking his cock at the rhythm of his hips thrusting into Mordred. Mordred bit the pillow he was clutching, but nothing could have stopped him from coming, not when he felt Amyas's thrusts stutter and his cock twitch and pulse inside his ass. He screwed his eyes shut and lost himself in the pleasure — into Amyas and the fact that they were one, if only for this moment.

"What are we doing?" Amyas murmured sometime later.

Mordred was on his back, with Amyas pressed against his side. He'd wrapped an arm around Amyas's shoulders to hold him close. Amyas wasn't going anywhere, but the thought of losing him was terrifying anyway.

"What do you mean?" Mordred asked as he stroked his fingertips up and down Amyas's naked back.

"Us. I've been staying in your bedroom almost since I arrived, and you just offered for me to move in completely. What does that mean?" Amyas paused and propped himself up on his elbow. He looked down at Mordred, and Mordred looked up at him. "You know I don't have any kind of experience with this. I've never had a relationship."

Mordred also knew why, but he still found it hard to believe. Amyas was young, even as an immortal being, but not *that* young. "Is that what you want? For us to be in a relationship?"

Amyas glared. "Isn't that what we already have? Or is it only sex?"

There was no way for Mordred to misread his own feelings, and they had nothing to do with only sex. "It's much more than that for me," he whispered.

Amyas watched him for a moment, then slowly nodded. "The same goes for me. This isn't only sex. When I asked you to take me along when you left the lake, I never thought something like this would happen."

"Is it a problem?" Amyas didn't look unhappy, but Mordred would do everything he could to change that if he was.

"How can you say that?" Amyas asked with a scowl. "Why would it be a problem? I'm just surprised. I didn't think it would happen, but it doesn't mean it's a bad thing."

"Even though you didn't want a relationship?" Mordred brushed strands of blond hair away from Amyas's face. He wanted to look at him while they had this conversation.

Amyas sighed. "I don't think I've ever not wanted a relationship. What I didn't want was to have one with someone I didn't know for the sake of getting a soul. What's between us is different."

"It is," Mordred agreed. He hesitated. He wasn't usually one to expose his feelings and talk about them, but this felt like the perfect time to do that. Amyas deserved to know what was going on, especially considering the life Mordred lived.

It was hard to kill a hero, but not impossible, and the conclave knew exactly how to do it. They wouldn't hesitate, either, if they got their hands on Mordred. Mordred didn't want to die without Amyas knowing how much he meant to him. He hoped that the way he behaved had already told him, but with Amyas, he couldn't know. Amyas was so used to being rejected and talked down to that he might not realize.

Mordred sucked in a breath. "I love you," he confessed.

Amyas didn't even look surprised, which made Mordred feel like a fool. Still, he smiled, and it helped.

"I love you, too," Amyas said as if it were the most natural thing in the world.

Maybe it was, at least between them.

Mordred pulled Amyas down into his arms, kissing him. It was getting late, and they should get to sleep, but Mordred wasn't sure he would be able to close his eyes with his chest feeling like it was bursting with happiness. "I love you," he repeated. He had a hard time believing he really had something this precious.

"And I love you, too," Amyas said, humor in his voice. "And I'll tell you again and again until you believe me."

"I already believe you."

Amyas leaned back, looking down at Mordred. "Are you sure? Because I know you don't believe you're worthy of this."

"You make me *want* to be worthy, and I think that's enough. We can work on our insecurities together."

Amyas huffed. "I want to tell you I don't have insecurities, but we would both know it's a lie. You're right, though. We can work on them together. We have time."

Mordred pulled Amyas closer again, and this time, Amyas settled against his chest. Mordred listened to his breathing until it softened and became more regular, a sure sign that Amyas was asleep. Mordred's eyelids were heavy and his eyes burned, but he wanted to enjoy this moment for just a bit longer.

Amyas was right, though. They had time to be together.

CHAPTER TEN

Mordred couldn't remember the last time he'd been humming as he worked. Probably never, now that he thought about it. This was what Amyas did to him. He made Mordred happy and feel like everything in the world was right, even though he was more than aware it wasn't.

He wasn't surprised when his phone rang. He'd known his peace wouldn't last forever, and he'd been expecting the conclave to do something. Since the name on his phone belonged to one of his spies, it seemed the peace was over.

"You shouldn't be calling," he scolded as he answered.

"I know. I had to, though."

It sounded urgent, so Mordred waited for his spy to explain what was going on.

"The conclave is sending a team to attack the tribe at the lake."

Mordred swore. "You're sure?"

The spy snorted. "Since I'm part of the conclave, I'm pretty sure, yes. I did my best to stop them, but I can't push too much, or they'll understand something is wrong."

"I'm aware. Dammit. I'm going to have to tell Amyas about this."

"I have to go."

"Wait. When are they attacking?"

"Tonight. I don't have the exact time yet, but I'll text you as soon as I know. It could be close."

"I'll have everyone ready to go. We'll make sure the undines make it out alive."

It wasn't going to be easy. Usually, undines just had to stick to their villages in their lake to make it, but Necsa had trained a team of warriors. They would attack, and it would be a bloodbath. Hopefully, that meant that at least the rest of the village would be fine, but Mordred couldn't swear to that.

He wasn't surprised that the worst aspect of the situation was having to tell Amyas what was happening. Amyas would freak out. Even though he was angry with his parents and his tribe, they were still his family, at least in part. He loved them, and he didn't want them to be hurt, especially not by heroes.

Mordred hung up and waited for a moment, but no text came through. Mordred snatched his phone and put it in his pocket before going to look for Amyas. The entire way there, he tried to find the best way to tell the man he loved that his family was in mortal danger. He doubted any way he could find would help ease Amyas into the situation. It was what it was, and instead of crying over it, they needed to act.

He wasn't surprised to find Amyas outside with Dimitri. They were at the small fountain, and Amyas's feet were in it again. Mordred would have to do something about that, because he wanted Amyas to have more than a fountain, but not right now.

They both turned to look at Mordred when they heard him, and Amyas beamed. "What are you doing here? I thought you were working."

"I was. I just got a phone call from my spy in the conclave."

"One day, you're going to have to tell me how you convinced whoever that is to move to our side," Dimitri said. "I'm curious, and I know Haven is, too. I also kind of want to get my hands on that person and strangle them for not helping Haven when the conclave almost executed him."

"I promise I'll tell you as soon as it's safe for the spy. Amyas, I have to talk to you."

That got Amyas's attention. He straightened, already

looking worried, and Mordred hated himself for what he had to do.

"What is it?" Amyas asked.

"The spy told me that the conclave is planning on attacking your village. It should happen tonight."

Amyas paled so much that Mordred found himself reaching for him in case he fainted. He didn't. Instead, he shook his head, tightening his hold on the stone bench he was sitting on until his knuckles were white. "What do you know?"

"Not much. My spy is going to text me as soon as they know more, but so far, they're sure the conclave will be sending a team tonight."

"You have to help them."

Mordred wasn't surprised Amyas was asking. "I was already planning on doing that."

"Even though they were going to kill you?"

"I can't blame Necsa for thinking all heroes are bad. I was at one time. I might even have been part of the team going to the lake. Supernatural beings have always viewed heroes like monsters because it's what most of them are."

"Not you and your team, though."

"Not me and my team," Mordred agreed.

But he couldn't deny at least to himself that he was tempted to say no, if anything, because Amyas would want to go along.

He couldn't. Amyas would never forgive him if he didn't go, especially since he had the resources to help. Besides, like Mordred had to tell himself again and again, Amyas could make his own decisions. Not being able to do that was the reason he'd left his parents, and Mordred didn't want to give him even one reason to leave him, too. Amyas was fiercely independent, which made sense after everything he'd gone through, and the last thing Mordred wanted was to clip his wings, even though thinking about Amyas being in the middle of the fight terrified him.

"Who's going?" Amyas said as he got to his feet.

"I have to see who's available, but since I still don't know how many heroes will be there, as many of us as possible."

"I'm going." Amyas looked at Mordred as if he expected Mordred to say no.

Mordred didn't blame him, since he'd been thinking about that only seconds before. "I'm going, too."

Amyas blinked. "Why? You usually stay here and keep everything under control from a distance."

"You really think I'm going to get let you go on your own? Besides, I used to go on these missions. I slowed down once I started recruiting more heroes, but it doesn't mean I never go on a mission. I wouldn't have met you if I hadn't."

Amyas nodded, looking down at his hands. "I'm scared."

Mordred moved to him, gathering him into his arms and hugging him close. "I know, and I can't promise you that everyone will make it out alive, but we're going to do our best. If Necsa is smart, she's going to keep everyone in the lake."

Amyas snorted against Mordred's chest. "She's smart, but she's also proud. She'll want to show the conclave she doesn't fear them and that she can stand up to them."

That was what Mordred had been afraid of. "Well, I hope she'll accept our help. If she tries to kill my men and me, we're going to have a problem."

"I think we should call Thor and Tryg," Dimitri said. He was on his feet, too, and he looked ready to run to Haven.

"We don't know if they're in the area," Mordred pointed out.

"We don't, but calling them would tell us, and they can help if they are. I have a feeling we're going to need all the help we can get."

Mordred had long dreamed of Tryg and Thor joining his organization. He knew Thor pretty well, and they'd worked together before, but Tryg had always been warier. He kept his distance, even more so now that he'd fallen in love. He had to protect his boyfriend, and Mordred understood. Still, having two draugr and possibly a mage if Thor's boyfriend wanted to be involved working along with the heroes would be incredible, both because they were capable and because it would show everyone they could work together. Having Dimitri and Amyas with them was the first step to do that. Mordred hoped more steps would happen in the future.

First, though, he had to take care of this problem. It wasn't going to be easy, but it wasn't the first hard mission they'd had to go on. All the heroes who worked with Mordred knew what they were going up against, and they weren't afraid of death or pain.

Amyas wasn't a hero, though. He might be immortal, but he could still die if he was wounded badly enough. Mordred could lose him, and if that happened, he didn't know what he would do.

Amyas had thought he was done with his family. It wasn't because he wanted to, but because he couldn't go back, and he knew his parents couldn't accept the fact that he didn't want a soul or to do what they thought he should do with his life.

What Mordred had said changed everything. Amyas couldn't stay away, not knowing that his parents and the village were going to be attacked today. He had to do something, but what? He wasn't a fighter. He was learning to be one, but it had only been a few weeks, and there was no way he was good enough to take on one hero, let alone a group of them. No, the village needed the heroes and not Amyas, but Amyas was going with them.

He wasn't surprised that Mordred didn't seem to have a

problem with it. He suspected that wasn't actually the case, but Mordred wouldn't say anything about it. He understood Amyas better than Amyas understood himself some days, and he knew Amyas wanted to make his own decisions, even though they might be stupid ones. Amyas couldn't stay away. He had to go with the heroes and make sure his family was okay.

He would also need to be the bridge between the heroes and the tribe, either before or after the fight. Hopefully, they would arrive before the conclave, but that meant Necsa would probably try to kill them. Amyas would have to stop her, and it wasn't going to be easy, knowing her.

"You need to promise me something," Mordred said as he, Amyas, and Dimitri walked toward the house.

Amyas wanted to tell him he didn't have to promise anything, but he realized he was only feeling this way because he was distressed. "What? I'm not staying here. I have to go with you."

"I know. That's why I haven't tried stopping you. But you have to be careful. I know Eudocia has been training you, but you only just started learning. Don't throw yourself into a fight you can't win. Stay back and let me and the heroes take care of it."

"I'm coming because I need to help the tribe, not to stay back and watch."

"No one is going to win if you get yourself killed."

"My life isn't a priority."

Mordred stopped walking, grabbed Amyas's arm, and moved them until they were facing each other. Then, he wrapped his fingers around both of Amyas's upper arms so Amyas couldn't step away. "Your life is a priority to *me*. If I have to choose, you always come first."

Amyas shook his head. "I can't come before your heroes and mission."

"You do. I don't know why it happened, but I love you, and I'm not going to let you sacrifice yourself, especially for people who don't deserve it. I'll do my best to protect the tribe and to make sure all of them make it out alive, but I need you to be careful. If you can't promise me that, I won't be able to focus on the fight. I'll be obsessed with finding out what's going on with you, and distraction is never a good thing when you're fighting."

Amyas wanted to protest, but he knew Mordred was telling the truth. They were in love. He needed to be honest, both with himself and Mordred. If he had to choose, Mordred would come first, too.

Amyas sucked in a breath. "I promise to be as careful as I can. I won't put myself in danger if I can avoid it, and I'll try my best to stay out of the worst fights. I do need to be there, though."

"I know. I understand."

They both heard Mordred's cell phone vibrate in his pocket. Amyas held his breath while Mordred took it out and looked at the screen.

"It's my contact. We have the time," Mordred said.

Everything after that went so quickly it made Amyas's head spin. The three of them went back to the house, and Mordred looked natural as he ordered people around. He managed to get all the heroes in the house to go to the living room and quickly explained what was going on while Amyas tried to contact his parents but didn't get an answer—which wasn't unexpected. Amyas was surprised that all the heroes volunteered for the mission, although maybe he shouldn't have been. They were his family now, and they wanted to help him.

A few of them had to stay back, but Mordred and Bayard were coming. It made Amyas feel better. He stuck close to Mordred as the heroes opened portals and stepped through. When his turn came, he hesitated. He was going to see his parents again, and they would no doubt try to convince him to stay after the fight. He already knew what his answer would be, but would they understand?

Mordred took Amyas's hand, raised it to his lips, and gently kissed the back of it. "You can still change your mind."

"I can't. I want to show my parents and Necsa that I can survive on my own and that I don't need a human or them."

"All right. Just remember that whatever they tell you, whatever you decide, you'll always have a home with us."

It didn't help as much as Amyas wanted it to, but when Mordred pulled him toward the portal, he went. Together, they stepped through, and Amyas blinked, looking around. He was back at the lake, the place he'd yearned to leave behind for so long. He'd managed, yet here he was, already back.

Everything was calm, and there was no trace of the conclave heroes yet. "I need to go to the lake to warn the tribe," Amyas said.

"Isn't there another way to do it?" Mordred asked.

"This is the fastest, since I can't contact them through water. I promise I'll be back. I won't change my mind when I see the village."

"I know. That's not what I was thinking."

"Well, stop worrying. Necsa will have a fight on her hands soon, and she'll have to focus on that. She won't care about me. She doesn't have a reason to, even though I was one of her tribe members. I'm not anymore, and she's probably happy she got rid of me. I was too much trouble."

Mordred kissed Amyas's forehead. "I'll be waiting for you here."

Amyas nodded and turned toward the lake. He was dressed in normal human clothes, which wasn't going to make the swim comfortable, but he didn't have a choice.

He let go of Mordred's hand and stepped into the lake. It

felt like he was back home, and he couldn't help but smile. He loved the lake and the water, just like every undine. He missed them now that he didn't have access to them, but he wouldn't give up what he had with Mordred and everything else for the lake. He could survive out of it, and he would. He would *thrive*.

He made his way to the village. Everything looked normal, which told him Necsa didn't know about the attack yet. Mordred wouldn't have known, either, if he hadn't had a contact in the conclave itself.

People started looking at him when he entered the village. He didn't stop. He went straight to Necsa's door, hoping she would listen to him.

"Amyas?"

Amyas almost groaned at the sound of his mother's voice. "I have something to do," he said.

She grabbed his arm and stopped him. "What are you doing here? I thought you were never coming back. That's what you said."

"It's temporary. I have to talk to Necsa."

"I'm your mother. You have to talk to me."

Amyas brushed his mother's hand off his arm. "We can talk later if you still want to. Right now, though, the village has to get ready."

"Ready for what?" his mother asked, obviously confused.

Amyas looked around. People had gathered, no doubt to find out what he was doing here and what he'd been up to since he'd left. Most of the people looking at him were whispering to each other, and he could imagine what they were saying.

None of that mattered. These people weren't ready for the attack, and they needed to be.

Amyas straightened. Necsa should be the one doing this, but since everyone was there, he would. "The lake is about to be attacked. The conclave sent heroes, and they're going to get here soon. I have to talk to Necsa so the village can get ready."

Mordred couldn't do anything but watch Amyas disappear into the lake. He desperately wanted to go with him, but he couldn't. His team needed him here, and going with Amyas would have created more problems—problems they didn't have the time to deal with. Besides, Mordred couldn't die by drowning, but it still wouldn't be pretty if he insisted on going with Amyas.

"What now?" Bayard asked. He was watching the lake, too.

"Now, we hope Amyas will be able to get through to his leader."

Bayard knocked their shoulders together. "*You're* his leader now."

It was still strange to think that. To Mordred, Amyas wasn't just one of his heroes, a member of the resistance. He was the man he loved, first and foremost.

Luckily for Mordred, he got the distraction he desperately needed when Thor and his boyfriend arrived. Cecil looked excited, while Thor looked worriedly at him. Thor made a beeline for Mordred after warning Cecil to be careful, which made Mordred smile, because he'd done the same with Amyas.

"You asked for help?" Thor asked when he reached Mordred.

Mordred rolled his eyes. "We can do this without you, but yeah. We're dealing with undines, which is where you come in."

Thor looked at the lake. "Do you want me to shift and go in there?"

"No. I just feel better having someone who can actually do

it. Amyas is down there right now, and I'm worried."

Thor stared at Mordred. "You know, it's funny how you expect me to know who Amyas is."

"I'm sure Dimitri told you." Haven and Thor were slightly closer than Thor was with Dimitri — which was strange since they'd been enemies until recently — but Mordred couldn't imagine Haven gossiping.

"He did. Well, he told Cecil, who told me. So you found yourself a boyfriend, huh?"

"Let's just say he found me."

Thor grinned. "I know about that, too. I can't believe you let yourself be captured."

"I don't mind it much since it means I met Amyas."

"I look forward to meeting him."

Mordred turned his attention to the lake again. "I hope you'll have that opportunity."

"In the meantime, why don't you tell me why we're here? Dimitri mentioned something about the conclave, but I'm sure you have more details."

Mordred was grateful for the distraction, and by the time he'd explained the little he knew about what was going on, Amyas was coming out of the lake. Mordred held his breath when he saw Amyas wasn't alone. He'd expected it, and it was why Amyas had insisted on going on his own, but it was still scary to see all the warriors surrounding him. Necsa was there, too, and she looked ready to kill Mordred, or even possibly Amyas if he said the wrong thing.

Thor whistled at the sight. "That's not something you see often," he murmured.

"These undines are . . . special." Mordred stepped forward. "Necsa," he said.

She stared at him. "Is what Amyas said true?"

"I'm not sure what he told you, but if he mentioned the conclave sending people, yes, it is."

"How do you know that?"

"I might not work for the conclave anymore, but it doesn't mean I don't have friends still with them. That's how I know. One of the people who gives me information I can use against the conclave let me know about it."

"And I'm supposed to believe you?"

"You don't have to. Do you really want to risk it, though?"

She crossed her arms over her chest. "The tribe can defend itself. You should know that. We captured you and your friend."

"Percival wasn't my friend." And Mordred suspected Percival would be here today. It would make sense for him to want revenge on Necsa.

Necsa waved her hand as if Mordred's words didn't matter. "Either way, we can defend ourselves. We don't need you to do it for us."

"You might think that, but you don't know the conclave. You and your village are fairly isolated. As long as you stay in the lake, the conclave can't touch you. You're insisting on fighting them, though, and it's not going to end well. That's why we're here. Because I knew you would react this way, and I want to avoid a bloodbath."

That was the wrong thing to say. Necsa bristled and straightened her shoulders, looking ready to fight Mordred here and now. Amyas was still by her side, but he noticed it, too, and he rushed to explain. "Mordred wants to help. That's what he and his people do, and they're the best people to do it, since they know the conclave. You should accept their help."

Necsa glared at Amyas. "Of course you think that. You ran away with him." She looked at Mordred again. "I want all of you to leave. If we *are* attacked, we'll take care of it on our own. We don't need you, and we don't want you here."

Mordred wasn't surprised. He hadn't expected anything

different from Necsa. The only reason he didn't have to decide whether or not to push and stay was that he and all the heroes around him felt a portal open nearby — a conclave portal.

Mordred looked at Bayard, who nodded grimly. "They're here," he confirmed.

Necsa took a step back and looked at the trees behind them. "Already?" she asked.

"What did you think, that the conclave was going to give you enough time to get ready? You're lucky I managed to get here in time. Otherwise, you wouldn't have known."

"It wouldn't have changed anything. We would have fought the conclave either way."

"We're not going anywhere. Even though you don't think you need our help, you do, and we're going to give it to you." Mordred owed it to Amyas. He was thinking of Amyas's parents and the people he loved. He didn't care if Necsa's pride was wounded. Pride was the worst thing to have when you were a leader. Better for her to learn it this way than by having her warriors decimated and her tribe eliminated.

Necsa turned to her warriors, giving quick orders. Mordred desperately wanted to grab Amyas and pull him closer, but he was surrounded by undines, and Mordred couldn't get to him, not without making how much he cared about him evident. They exchanged a glance, and Amyas smiled, no doubt trying to reassure Mordred. Unfortunately, it didn't work. Mordred suspected he was always going to worry about Amyas, but if he truly wanted Amyas to be safe, he needed to focus on the fight that was about to happen. Amyas had promised he would be careful, and Mordred had to believe him.

Then Mordred didn't have any more time to think about Amyas and what was happening. The small shore they were standing on flooded with heroes, and the fight began.

It was Mordred's element. He was used to this, and he found himself feeling at home fighting heroes. Fighting was always both terrifying and exhilarating. It could mean death, or at the very least for heroes, painful wounds. It was always scary, but especially so now that Amyas was in the picture. Mordred had to force himself to focus on what was happening around him rather than looking for Amyas and trying to help him. Amyas wouldn't thank him for that, and Mordred wanted to go home to Amyas once this was over.

He wouldn't if he didn't put all he had in the fight.

Just like Amyas had told Mordred, he wasn't defenseless. He mostly knew what he was doing thanks to Eudocia, but even he was surprised at how good he'd become at fighting once the heroes arrived. Defending himself and kicking ass was exhilarating.

It was also terrifying, though.

Even though Amyas was doing his best, it was obvious he didn't have experience in fighting. It made him an easy target, but luckily for him, the former conclave heroes fighting around him seemed to take special care in keeping him safe. They didn't say anything about it, just knocked down the heroes trying to hurt Amyas before going back to their own fights. Amyas was grateful, but at the same time, it made him feel useless. He'd insisted on coming because he'd wanted to make sure his parents were safe, but maybe it had been a mistake. Maybe he should have stayed home with Eudocia and the other few heroes with her. It would have made more sense. If he weren't here, the heroes wouldn't have to keep him safe, too.

It was too late to go back. Everything was a mess, and Amyas knew he'd always remember his first fight. It made him wonder if this really was what he wanted to do with his life, but now wasn't the best time to think about it. He had to focus on not getting killed, and it wasn't as easy to do as he wished.

He didn't see the sword coming. He should have, but he was distracted, and he was lucky he wasn't killed on impact. Someone cried out, though, and he turned. He noticed the glint of metal and threw himself to the side. The bite of pain in his arm made him cry out. He stumbled and fell on the ground, blood pouring out of his arm. He felt sick at the sight, and he looked around for help.

His stomach heaved, and he tried getting back to his feet. Strong hands grabbed him and helped him, and he prayed his helper wasn't a conclave hero. If it had been a conclave hero, they would have been trying to finish him instead of helping him.

An undine warrior stood over him. He pushed Amyas toward the lake, his expression grim. "You need to get that seen by a healer."

"I have to stay and fight."

"You're not doing a good job of it. You're going to get yourself or someone else killed if you stay."

The bottom of Amyas's stomach dropped. "I didn't mean to do that."

"What you meant to do doesn't matter. Go. The healers will help you."

He was right. Amyas wasn't in this on his own, and he had to be careful. He had to make sure the people he loved and cared about made it out alive, and if that meant taking himself out of the fight, he would do it. If Mordred noticed he was wounded, he would freak out, and that was the last thing Amyas wanted. Mordred had to focus on the fight and on doing what was right, not on Amyas.

That was why Amyas allowed the undine to drag him into the lake. He didn't stay with him long, though. Amyas knew where to go anyway, and he watched the warrior swim back to the surface, ready to throw himself into the fight again.

Amyas felt terrible about what had happened, but there was nothing he could do about it. Instead of swimming back to the surface like he wanted, he turned around and headed toward the village. He wasn't surprised to see his parents there, waiting along with most of the village. They were frantic, and his mother cried out when she saw him. "What happened to you?" she asked.

"Nothing. I'm fine."

"You're not fine." She hovered her hands above the wound on Amyas's arm.

It hurt, but he did his best not to let it show. He didn't want his parents to tell him they'd told him so, even though they had, in a way. "I'm fine," he repeated.

"You're bleeding," his father pointed out.

"I know. I'll be fine, though. It's just a small wound." Even though Amyas's arm felt like it was about to fall off.

"Let's get you to the healer," his father answered. "How are things going up there?"

"I'm not sure."

"We're winning, of course," his mother said.

"You can't know that," his father gently said, but it was obvious both to him and Amyas that Amyas's mother wasn't going to listen.

She was convinced Necsa would save them all, and maybe she would. What would happen if she didn't, though? Amyas couldn't think about that right now, because if Necsa lost, it meant Mordred had, too. The thought was too horrifying for Amyas to allow himself to think about it, so instead, he focused on the pain.

That was surprisingly easy.

Several healers were waiting, and Amyas was relieved. He was one of the few wounded right now, so they could focus on him, which meant he would be able to go back to the surface soon. He might not be much help, but he *could* help, and that was all that mattered. He didn't care what the warriors or his parents said. He was part of this, and he wasn't going to allow anyone to keep him here.

"Can you give me something for the pain?" he asked.

The healer nodded. "I was planning on doing that anyway. It will probably knock you out, though."

"I can't. I have to go back."

The healer looked skeptical. "You can't. You're wounded, and you're not a fighter."

That was one of the problems of growing up in a place where everyone knew everyone. "I'll be fine," Amyas tried to insist.

"You won't. You're doing something stupid, but I'm not surprised. What I *am* surprised at is that Necsa allowed it."

"I'm not part of this village anymore. She can't forbid me to do anything."

The healer exchanged a glance with Amyas's parents.

Amyas gritted his teeth. He knew what that glance meant. They didn't think he was able to do this, and maybe they were right. Amyas would die trying, though. He wasn't useless, and he wanted people to see that, but more importantly, he wanted to *help*. Mordred was out there, fighting for the tribe even though the tribe would gladly kill him if they could. The least Amyas could do was to help him, and he was planning on doing just that.

"All right," the healer said. "I won't give you anything that will knock you out. Stay here. I'll be back soon with what I need to help you."

Amyas eyed the bag the healer had been working from. "Don't you have what you need in there?"

"Not if you don't want painkillers that might knock you out. You're sure about this?"

"I am," Amyas said. It hurt, but he could deal with it. He *had* to deal with it.

"Stay here, then. I'll be right back."

He nodded and watched the healer leave the infirmary he'd been led into. He turned his attention to his parents, but they were quietly talking to each other, and they stopped as soon as they saw he noticed them. "I can't believe you're doing this," Amyas's mother said. "You put yourself in danger, and you almost got killed. Is this really what you want to do with your life? You could be married and having children, and you could have a soul, but instead, this is what you want?"

Amyas wasn't up for this conversation. "I'm not changing my mind. I want to do this, and I will."

His mother pressed a hand against her mouth and got to her feet. "I can't listen to this. Seeing my own son trying to end his life this way. I can't." She rushed toward the door, and Amyas's father got to his feet, too.

"I'm going to go after her," he explained.

Amyas was already exhausted by all of this. He nodded, hoping his father could talk some sense into his mother. "Sure. I'm not going anywhere."

"You're right. You're not," Amyas's father agreed.

The words were weird, and Amyas watched his father move toward the door. His father gave him one last glance, then he stepped outside and closed the door behind himself.

Amyas heard the door lock. He straightened, already panicking, and got to his feet. "Dad?" he called out.

"We're doing this for you," his father explained.

"What are you talking about? What are you doing?"

"Necsa agreed with this. She said that we should keep you here if we could, and that's what we're doing. You'll be fine. The tribe will take care of you, and we'll find you a good wife."

"I don't want a wife," Amyas yelled. "I want to go back to Mordred. I want to help him."

"You can't. You'll stay here until you change your mind."

"I won't change my mind."

"Necsa will take care of it. We love you, Amyas. That's why we're doing this. You should rest. You lost blood, and it's not good for you."

Amyas screamed at his father, but he could hear footsteps fading, which meant his father wasn't standing there anymore. He listened, but the only thing he could hear on the other side of the door was silence.

They'd locked him up in the infirmary. Amyas was a prisoner to his own parents, to his tribe.

He pushed away from the door and went to sit on the bed again. He couldn't believe his parents had done this to him. They knew he wasn't happy, yet they didn't seem to care.

That wasn't the most important thing right now, though. The most important thing was Mordred and how he was doing, and Amyas wondered when Mordred would notice he was gone and what the man he loved would do once he did.

CHAPTER ELEVEN

Fighting was always exhilarating. Mordred supposed most people would think him strange, but the heroes wouldn't. This was what they were born for, and it was what they did best.

He wasn't sure how many heroes the conclave had sent, but they clearly hadn't expected the response they'd gotten. Together, the former heroes and the tribe managed to push back the conclave heroes. Several were already opening portals to run away, and it made Mordred grin savagely.

He punched a hero on the nose, kicked another between the legs, and watched as both tried to get to the portal. "Tell the conclave we won't allow them to hurt more people," he yelled after them.

"The conclave will have your head for this," another hero yelled.

Mordred's smile widened when he saw it was Percival. "You really think they would have come to save you?" he asked. He knew they wouldn't have. "They would have let Necsa kill you without a thought."

Percival shrugged. "And I would have deserved to die. I should have, since I was weak enough to allow the undines to capture me."

His sword crossed with Mordred's. Mordred didn't want to kill Percival. He still hoped he would eventually get through to him, even though it didn't seem likely right now.

Mordred never enjoyed killing other heroes. He always felt like it was a lost opportunity to bring someone to his side, and more importantly, to make them see how wrong the conclave was. He wasn't going to hesitate if Percival tried to kill him, though.

Percival lunged, trying to stab his sword into Mordred's guts. He was young, though, and while he no doubt had experience fighting, Mordred had more of it. He sidestepped the sword, causing Percival to stumble forward, and used the hilt of his weapon to hit Percival on the back of the head. Percival dropped like a sack of rocks, and Mordred stood above him, wondering what to do with him. He'd wanted Percival to listen, but the man couldn't do that while he was unconscious.

He looked around. Percival was the only hero left. The others had disappeared through portals, and they wouldn't come back for him.

A warrior came closer, intent on killing Percival. Mordred couldn't allow him to do that, though, and he raised his sword. "Step back," he ordered.

"He attacked us. He killed my brothers," the warrior said.

"I don't care. Step back, or I'll make you."

"You should listen to him," Thor said as he came closer. He crouched behind Percival and turned him around. "You got him good. He's unconscious."

"I know." Mordred looked around and noticed Bayard coming toward them. He gestured at Percival, and Bayard nodded. "Bayard will take care of him. He won't be hurt," he repeated so the warrior knew where he stood. Then Mordred dismissed him, even though the warrior was still protesting. He looked around, needing to find Amyas.

He couldn't.

No matter how hard he looked, how long he did so, he couldn't see Amyas anywhere. He asked several people, and while a few were able to tell him that Amyas had been wounded, none could say where he was.

"Take your people and go," Necsa said, stepping in front

of Mordred.

"I won't go without Amyas. Where is he? What did you do with him?" Because Mordred was sure Necsa had something to do with this.

Amyas would never have left of his own accord. He'd wanted to be here to help his people, but he also wanted to go home with Mordred. Mordred was sure of that, and he wasn't going to doubt Amyas. He *could* doubt Necsa, though, which was exactly what he was doing.

She glared at him. "Where Amyas is or isn't is none of your business. The fight is over, and while I thank you for what you did, I won't hesitate to attack if you don't go."

"I want Amyas back."

"He's an undine. He belongs here, with us, not with you."

"He doesn't *want* to be with you."

"He'll change his mind. He'll come to realize that his parents and I were right, and he wasn't. He doesn't need you. He needs *us*, and we're going to take care of him."

"What have you done to him? He would never agree to stay here with the tribe if you hadn't done something to him. If you hurt him—"

"We won't. You did, though. He was wounded. He stupidly thought he could fight, and he was wrong."

"He can do anything he wants, and that includes fighting."

"You were stupid to allow him to come. Now go, before I order my warriors to attack you and your people."

Mordred tightened his hands into fists and resisted the urge to attack her. He wanted to tear her head off her shoulders, and he could. As strong as she was, he was a hero. They were both immortal, but she was more vulnerable, and he would gladly kill her if it gave him Amyas back.

A hand grabbed his shoulder and pulled him back. "We should go," Thor murmured.

"I can't leave Amyas here."

"I know. It's only temporary." He looked at Necsa. "You're making a mistake, and you know it. Amyas doesn't want to stay here with you. You won't be able to keep him prisoner forever."

"He'll change his mind once he's away from you. You're the only reason he decided to leave the lake. You brainwashed him, and we'll make sure you can't do that anymore."

Mordred wanted to scream. He wanted to tell Necsa she was a liar. He knew it wouldn't help, though. As much as he hated it, Thor was right—they had to leave.

Fighting the undine warriors wouldn't help anyone, least of all Amyas. There was no way for Mordred and the others to know what was going on under the water. Hurting Necsa might hurt Amyas, too, and that was the last thing Mordred wanted.

"This isn't over," he warned Necsa.

She shrugged, clearly not believing him. "We'll see."

"I won't allow you to force Amyas into anything."

"I'm not. He's an undine, and his goal in life should be to get a soul, something you can't give him. Now go. We already talked for too long, and I have to take care of my people. You should do the same, too, and forget about Amyas. He'll forget about you soon enough."

She turned around and walked into the lake. Her warriors followed, some limping, others helping the wounded in an upright position. Mordred stayed where he was until the last undine had disappeared into the water.

"We'll get him back," Thor promised.

"I know. I won't rest until he's home with me," Mordred said.

It was a promise, even though there was no one there to hear it.

Mordred hoped Amyas wouldn't believe anything Necsa said when it came to him. Even if she tried telling him

Mordred had left him behind, he would know that wasn't the truth. He knew Mordred and his friends would get him back.

Mordred had to cling to that knowledge, too. Amyas was aware of what was happening, and he knew Mordred would be back for him. He only had to wait. Mordred couldn't, though. He had to do something, and he had to do it as soon as possible. Amyas was wounded, and Mordred had to see that he was okay with his own two eyes. That wasn't going to happen until he got Amyas back, but there was nothing else he could do.

He turned toward Thor and the other heroes. "Let's go home. We have to start planning."

Everyone looked grim, but they also all nodded. They were with Mordred, and they would be with him until they had Amyas back. It didn't matter that Amyas was an undine while they weren't. He was family, and to them, family was everything.

To Mordred, *Amyas* was everything.

Amyas was pissed. He'd never imagined his parents would do something like this. From Necsa, he could see it. From his parents, though?

Maybe he *should* have seen it coming, though. He'd known they weren't happy he was staying with Mordred and that they'd wished he would stay home. They'd wanted him to come back, and now they had what they wished for. Amyas wasn't going to allow them to do this without complaining, though. He wasn't staying here, and that was that. He didn't know how he would manage to leave, but he'd find a way.

He had to.

He had to go back to Mordred. Mordred was the only one who had ever treated Amyas like an adult who could make his own decisions. Amyas had been afraid he wouldn't when he'd declared he was coming along, but even though Mordred had clearly been unhappy with the decision, he hadn't demanded Amyas stay home. He'd agreed to let him come, and he'd respected Amyas and the decisions he made.

Amyas's parents didn't. No matter what they said or what they wanted, Amyas wasn't staying. He didn't know how to leave, though.

He looked around. His arm hurt, but at least the healer had taken care of it before locking him into the room. Now that Amyas knew what had been happening, the glances between the woman and his parents made sense. They'd been planning this all along, and Amyas hadn't seen it.

He was in the infirmary, and there wasn't much he could use to leave. The door was locked, and all the windows had bars. They didn't have glass, since they didn't need it under the water, but the bars helped keep fish and other things that swam in the lake out of the infirmary and the other buildings in the village. Amyas wouldn't be leaving that way or through the door.

Where would he be leaving from, then?

He swallowed. He couldn't see a way out of this, but he wasn't giving up. He was in love with Mordred, and that was enough to keep him going. He wasn't sure how long he'd been there when someone unlocked the door. He shot to his feet, grimacing at the pain in his arm but doing his best to ignore it.

The door swung open, and Necsa stepped in.

Amyas had to remember she wasn't his leader anymore. "What are you doing?" he asked.

Necsa didn't look surprised at his defiant tone. She stepped in, followed by Amyas's parents.

He ignored them. He understood why Necsa was doing it, but he would never forgive his parents for it. "Let me go," he said.

"Why would you want to go? You belong here with us," Necsa said.

"I don't. I belong wherever I decide I belong, and it's not here."

"It's a pity your friends left, then."

The bottom of Amyas's stomach dropped. He didn't think Necsa was lying—she wasn't a liar, at least not usually. That meant that Mordred and the others *had* left, just like she said. Amyas didn't want to believe her, but he did. There had to be a good explanation. Necsa could have threatened to hurt him if he and the others didn't go. That was exactly the kind of thing she would do. "What did you tell him to make him leave?" he asked.

Necsa shook her head. "It doesn't matter. They won't be coming back. They left you with us, and you're going to stay."

"I don't want to," he snapped. "You can't force me to stay. I'm not one of your tribe members anymore."

"You're an undine," Necsa answered in the same tone. "You were born here, in this village, and you grew up here. You belong with us. If you don't want to stay, you'll have to find a human and marry them. That's the only opportunity you'll have to leave the village. If you refuse, you'll stay with us."

"You can't force me to stay. Are you going to keep me locked up all my life?"

"If I have to. I'm sure it won't come to that. Eventually, you'll understand. You'll come to see that your parents and I are right and that we only want what's best for you. Until then, you'll stay here."

"Aren't you going to need the infirmary?"

"We do. That's why you'll be moved into a cell."

"Mordred won't stand back and watch you do this. He'll intervene."

"And if he does, I'll have him killed. You know better than

to go against me, Amyas. I hope you told that to your friend. He needs to know what will happen if he tries to get to you. I think I got through to him when I told him to leave, but if I didn't, well, I'll deal with it when he comes." She watched Amyas for a moment. "Why would he come back anyway?"

"Because he loves me."

"He's a hero, and you're a supernatural being. He can't love you. He probably told you that to get what he wanted, and I'm sure he did. You were always weaker than I'd have liked you to be, but now, things will change. I'll keep an eye on you until you understand. Until then, you won't be able to leave the cell you'll be locked in."

She didn't wait for Amyas to answer. She turned around, striding to the door, and even though Amyas called out for her, she didn't stop. He hadn't expected her to. If he was honest, he didn't want to talk to her. He knew that nothing he could say would make her change her mind. She *couldn't* change her mind because she was too proud. She didn't want people to see her as weak and as someone who gave up.

He sighed and turned to his parents. "How could you do this to me?"

Amyas's mother reached for him, but he took a step back. He didn't want her to touch him. She looked hurt, but thankfully, she didn't insist. "We only want what's best for you," she said.

"If you truly wanted what's best for me, you'd let me make my own choices. You wouldn't force me to be here when I don't want to be." Amyas could see how much his words hurt his mother, but he couldn't bring himself to care.

"Eventually, you'll understand," Amyas's father said. He took Amyas's mother's hand and pulled her toward the door. "Just remember that we both love you. We'll welcome you back home once you're ready."

Amyas looked around for something to throw at his

parents, but he couldn't find anything quickly enough. They stepped through the door, and it closed behind them, leaving Amyas to stare at it.

He was alone again, and he had answers. What he didn't have was a way out of this.

Mordred had left, but he would be back. Amyas was sure of that. What was he going to do, though? Mordred couldn't get to Amyas, not while Amyas was in the lake, and if he couldn't get to him, how would he get him out of here?

He couldn't. That meant Amyas would have to find a way to save himself. He'd never done it before, and the thought was terrifying. He was ready to do that and much more to get back to Mordred, though. No matter what Necsa had said, Amyas knew that Mordred hadn't abandoned him. He would be back for Amyas, and he would do whatever he could to get to him. It wasn't going to be easy, but they *would* find a way back to each other.

Chapter Twelve

"We have to go get him," Mordred said through gritted teeth. He didn't want to yell, but he felt he was on the brink of doing just that. "It's already been an entire day. Who knows what they're doing to him?"

He was surprised when Dimitri reached for his arm and squeezed. "I know you're worried," Dimitri said. "We all are. We can't rush into this, though. We'd risk him and us getting hurt, and he wouldn't want that."

"Besides, I doubt they're doing anything bad to him," Bayard intervened. "They're his people, even though he left them behind. They want him to come back to them, not to hurt him. You heard what Necsa said."

Mordred forced himself to breathe. They were right. He would have known that if he'd been able to think, but he wasn't, not with Amyas in danger. He'd known he was in love with Amyas before, but the force of his feelings was surprising even to him. The thought of being without Amyas made him want to weep, and it was a miracle he wasn't crying in front of his friends.

He needed to be strong, both for them and for Amyas.

"What's the plan?" he asked after he finally managed to get his fear under control.

"We have to be smart about it," Thor said.

Mordred looked around the table. He trusted every single person who was sitting there with him. Dimitri and Haven were there, as were Thor and his boyfriend. Bayard and Eudocia were the last ones, but Thor had told Mordred that Tryg and Isaac were coming. Mordred suspected he didn't want to make a move until they got here, and he tended to agree when he thought about it.

The problem was that he wasn't thinking clearly. He had to force himself to do it, because thinking clearly was the only way he would get Amyas back in one piece. He was already hurt. Mordred didn't want anything else to happen to him.

"Are you sure he didn't just decide to stay with the tribe?" Thor asked. It was the first time Mordred heard him talk that hesitantly.

"He didn't. He left his village because he wanted to be free to make his own decisions. They never allowed him to, and I'm sure that's the case once again. They're holding him prisoner, and I won't stand for that." It took everything Mordred had not to snap his answer, and he had to remind himself that Thor didn't know Amyas.

"None of us will. As soon as Tryg and Isaac are here, we can plan our next step. I have a few ideas, but I want to talk them out with Tryg first."

Mordred wanted to protest, but he didn't. Thor was probably his only chance to get to Amyas. Amyas was at the bottom of the lake, and even though Mordred couldn't drown, he also couldn't spend that much time in the water. That meant someone else had to get to Amyas, and both Thor and Tryg could shift into seals. They were the only ones present who could do that, and Mordred had to remind himself of it.

Bayard's phone rang, and he looked at the screen. He frowned and stepped to the side of the room to answer while Mordred and the others continued talking about Amyas. Everyone believed he was being kept in the lake against his will, for which Mordred was grateful. He didn't know what he would have done if he'd had to convince them of that, too.

"Mordred?" Bayard said.

His voice was enough to make Mordred look up. His tone

was urgent and worried, and it didn't bode well. "Yes?"

Bayard held his phone out. "It's the conclave. They want to talk to whoever is in charge."

Mordred got to his feet. He hadn't expected this, but it would be a good distraction from Amyas and what was happening to him. Mordred had to remember that he was working against the conclave and that they'd just fought against them. Amyas would want him to focus on that instead of him, and while that wasn't possible, Mordred could give it at least half an hour.

"Yes?" he asked when he answered.

"Mordred. I knew I'd hear from you again when you left us," a voice drawled.

Mordred suddenly wanted to punch something. He sucked in a breath, knowing he couldn't show Ceara any kind of weakness. She'd trained him, and she knew him well. She would zero in on that and use it to her advantage. "I should have known you would try to contact me," he answered.

"Probably. You were never very bright, though."

"I was bright enough to see what the conclave was doing and to get away from you. I'm bright enough to challenge and fight you." And he was winning, but he didn't add that. He didn't want to get her angry, not yet, not when he didn't know what she wanted.

"Let's get to the point," she said briskly. She wasn't happy with his answer.

He understood why. She'd trained him herself, and they'd been close while he'd worked with the conclave. She'd tried to mold him into what she thought of as the perfect warrior, and she'd failed. Mordred had taken everything she'd taught him and had used it to fight her. He suspected she hated him and that she would gladly kill him if she ever managed to get her hands on him.

"I'm listening," he told her.

"The conclave wants you and your heroes to stay out of the way. You're ruining our mission."

Mordred snorted. "You mean we're ruining your plans. The heroes' mission was to protect both human beings and paranormal beings against the bad ones. You warped that, and you're using the heroes to your advantage instead of doing what's right."

"How did I not see how stupid you were when I trained you?"

Mordred ignored Ceara's snark. "The heroes are supposed to protect everyone, and that includes innocent supernatural beings."

"Supernatural beings are the ones putting people in danger. Have they brainwashed you?"

"No, but the conclave sure tried. You won't change my mind or the mind of the heroes who are working with me. We know what we're doing, and we're convinced of it. I don't care what you offer us or how you threaten us. We won't stop."

"That's all I needed to hear. Remember that if you don't stop opposing us, we won't hesitate to kill you, even though you worked with us at one time."

"You mean we worked *for* you. You manipulated us, and we've had enough. We're standing up to you and the entire conclave now, and we'll continue doing so until you go back to doing what you were supposed to do from the beginning."

"If I can, I'll kill you myself. I'll make sure your people, your fallen heroes, are there to watch. And once they've seen you die, they will have the same fate. You know how powerful the conclave is. We won't stand back and let you do what you want."

"Strange, because you've been doing it for a while now. Do you even know where I am?"

"I don't need to know where you are. Eventually, you *will*

surrender yourself to me. When that happens, I'll make sure your death is as painful as possible."

She hung up, leaving Mordred to stare at the screen of the phone.

He had no doubt she'd been telling the truth when she'd threatened him. It was nothing new, though. Even though this was the first time the conclave actively tried to contact Mordred, thanks to his spy amongst them, he knew what was said during their meetings. They'd wanted to get rid of Mordred and his fallen heroes since the beginning. They wouldn't stop for anything to make it happen.

It was a good thing Mordred was stubborn. He would continue standing up to the conclave and doing what was right, even if it meant getting killed.

First, though, he was going to get Amyas back.

Amyas was still angry, even though a day had passed. The only person who had come to see him in his new cell was the healer, and she'd only checked his arm and given him food. Neither his parents nor Necsa had come around, which was a pity, because Amyas would have enjoyed yelling at them. It wouldn't have achieved much, but he would probably feel better if he'd been able to tell everyone just how angry he was.

He'd examined the cell he was in in the hope of finding a weakness he could use to run away, but he hadn't found any. He wasn't giving up, but he was starting to feel nervous about his plan.

He had to save himself. Mordred couldn't come to him because he was at the bottom of the lake. *No one* could come to him, which meant Amyas had to save himself.

How was he supposed to do that? He'd allowed his anger to power him, but now it was fading, and he didn't know if he would be able to go on without it.

Every time he heard a sound outside the cell, Amyas straightened and glared at the door. Usually, the footsteps faded, but this time, they didn't. He didn't get up from the bed he was sitting on. When the door opened, his glare deepened.

His parents stepped in. They looked wary, and they were right to be.

"Amyas. We came to see how you were feeling," his mother said.

"How do you think I'm feeling? You locked me up. You're keeping me here against my will. You kidnapped me and are keeping me *prisoner*."

Amyas's father blanched, but his mother didn't seem to care about his words. "You know it was the right thing to do," she insisted. "It's better this way because you can finally find a nice human and marry her."

Amyas resisted the urge to punch the wall—it wouldn't have helped. "I don't want to find a nice human, and I don't like females that way."

"A man, then."

Amyas shook his head. His mother would never listen to him. She wanted this to happen, and she would focus only on that until it did. It didn't matter what Amyas said or felt. She had her own idea in mind, and that was all that mattered to her.

Amyas didn't regret coming to help the tribe fight the heroes, but now that he knew that his parents would never accept him the way he was, he wished he hadn't. He wouldn't have been in this situation if he'd stayed home.

Home. For all his life, it had been this village. It wasn't anymore, though, and he yearned for the huge house and Mordred, for all the friends he'd made there. He wanted to go back, but he didn't know how to do that.

"What your mother is saying is that now that you're back,

we can sit down and talk about what you want," Amyas's father said. "I know we haven't always given you what you needed, but we're ready to listen to you."

Amyas snorted. "Yeah? Because to me, it doesn't look like you are. You keep telling me this is for the best, and now, you want to listen to me, yet you haven't been." He got to his feet, but he stayed away from his parents. He didn't want them to try to touch him. "I want to go back to Mordred. I'm in love with him, and I'm not going to marry anyone else."

"It will pass," Amyas's mother said. "Marriage isn't about love. It's about who's best for you, and it's not Mordred. I know it hurts, but the feelings will fade, and you'll feel better."

"See? That's what I was talking about," Amyas said, looking at his father. "You're *not* listening. Neither you nor Mom are. You only hear what you want to hear, and you don't have my happiness in mind. I don't think you ever did. You want me to do what *you* decide I should do, and that's not going to happen."

"Necsa is going to keep you here until you agree," Amyas's father said.

"Then she's going to have to keep me here for a long time, because I'm not changing my mind."

Amyas's father sighed. "It's what I was afraid of. We're going to check your wound. Then we'll go. You obviously need more time to think."

This time, Amyas didn't resist the urge. He slapped his hand against the wall, making both his parents jump. He felt a savage satisfaction at the way they were looking at him as if they didn't know him. They didn't, and they never had. They didn't want to admit it, but they had no idea who Amyas was and what he wanted. "You don't have to check my wounds. I'm fine. If you're not here to help me, you know where the door is. I don't want to see you again."

"We're your parents," his mother tried.

"You might be, but it doesn't mean you're my family. It doesn't mean you care about me. If you did, you'd let me go. You would let me do what I want with my life instead of insisting that what you want is the right choice."

"We do care about you. You're our son, and you're young. You still need guidance, and what you're saying proves that."

Amyas raked a hand through his hair, his fingers catching on several tangles. He pulled on it, enjoying the pain because it reminded him that this was only momentary. He would go home soon, and he would never have to talk to his parents again. "Just go. I don't want to see you or to talk to you. If you don't have to listen to me, then I don't have to listen to you." He didn't want to hear what they were saying. He didn't care what they thought, not as long as they kept him here.

He stretched out on the bed, turning his back to them. He heard them talk quietly for a few moments, then their footsteps moving toward the door. It opened, then closed, and Amyas was alone again.

He'd never been this alone. He'd only been in this cell one day, and he was already bored and freaking out. What would happen if he had to stay longer? If he had to stay here weeks, or even months?

Amyas was sure that Mordred was trying to find a way to get to him, but would he? Amyas had faith in Mordred, but Mordred wasn't an undine. He couldn't swim and get to the bottom of the lake, even though he was immortal. Amyas needed to find a way out on his own, but he hadn't managed yet, and he wasn't sure he would. Besides, even though he was angry, he didn't want a war between Mordred and the tribe. That was what would happen if Mordred tried to get to Amyas. Necsa had made sure Amyas knew what she would do to Mordred if she ever got her hands on him.

Right now, Amyas didn't like Necsa. He'd never hated her

as a leader, even though he sometimes thought she was too focused on her own feelings instead of what would be best for the tribe. This was just another sign that pointed to that. He was angry, but in this situation, she held all the cards, and he didn't have any. If he wanted out of the cell, he was going to have to act as if he agreed with what she said. The problem was that if he did now, she would know he was lying. She would understand why he was doing it, and she wouldn't fall for it.

Amyas flopped onto his back and stared at the ceiling. He wasn't giving up, even though it was hard. What he had with Mordred and the other fallen heroes was worth trying, no matter how many times he had to do it. Eventually, he would find a way out of this situation, and he would go home to Mordred and his friends.

He looked around again. He'd already walked around the cell more than once, trying to find a way out, but even though he hadn't, he got to his feet to do it one more time. It was the only thing he could do, and it was better than lying on the bed wondering when everything had gone so wrong.

Tryg and Isaac had finally arrived. Mordred realized it had only been a day since he'd last seen Amyas, but it felt like an eternity. He'd slept alone for hundreds of years, yet his bed had never felt as empty as it had last night, without Amyas in it. He wanted Amyas back, and he hoped that now that Tryg and Isaac were here, Thor would finally agree to do something. Logically, Mordred understood why Thor had wanted to wait. Emotionally, though, he was a wreck, and he needed to do *something*. It didn't even matter what at this point. He was ready to swim to the village himself if it got Amyas back.

"Ready?" Bayard asked as he appeared at the door of Mordred's office.

Mordred was already on his feet, and he rushed toward his second. "They're in the small meeting room?"

"They are. Thor walked them there, and he quickly explained what's going on. Everyone is ready to talk and find a solution."

"It's about time," Mordred grumbled. He was aware of how lucky he was that so many people were willing to help him and cared about Amyas. It didn't help much when it came to not freaking out about what was going on with Amyas right now, though. Mordred hoped Necsa wasn't hurting him, but he couldn't be a hundred percent sure.

She'd said she wanted the best for Amyas, but that was a lie. The best for Amyas was something only Amyas could decide, and Necsa couldn't see that. Would she push to the point of hurting Amyas if he kept on telling her where to stuff it? Mordred wanted to say no, but could he be sure?

He didn't know Necsa well, but what he did know about her made him nervous. She was used to being obeyed, and Amyas was putting a monkey wrench in that. He was showing the rest of the tribe that she could be disobeyed, and she didn't like that. She might lose her patience, which was the last thing Mordred wanted to happen. If she did, she could hurt Amyas, and Mordred wouldn't be there to help him.

He followed Bayard to the meeting room. Just like Bayard had said, most of the people meeting with them were already there. Thor and Tryg were sitting next to each other with their heads close as they talked quietly. Dimitri, Cecil, and Isaac were also sitting together, and they were talking, too. Haven was keeping himself separate, but Mordred had no doubt he was listening to whatever was being said in both the conversations. Then, there was Eudocia. For whatever reason, she seemed amused. She was also listening, and she smiled kindly when she noticed Mordred walk into the room. "We're ready," she said.

Mordred could have kissed her for being his friend and being so nice. Instead, he sat in his chair at the head of the table and looked down its length. "Welcome," he told Isaac and Tryg.

Tryg huffed, but Isaac smiled kindly. "We're here to help," he said.

"Good, because I *need* your help."

"Can you tell us what happened?"

Mordred frowned. "I'm sure Thor already told you."

"He did, but he didn't explain a few things, and I'm curious. I understand why you want to get Amyas back, but why is he so important to you? He's an undine after all, and he does belong in the lake with his people."

Mordred glared at Thor. "You didn't tell them?"

Thor shrugged. "I didn't think it was my place."

"You could have told them. It would have made this faster."

"Stop grumbling and tell them yourself."

Mordred sucked in a breath. "Amyas is important to me because I love him."

There was a moment of silence, and Mordred expected to be judged. He should have known better, though. He wasn't friends with Isaac or Tryg, but he knew them, and he knew they would have nothing to say about what he'd just explained.

In fact, Isaac limited himself to nod thoughtfully. "I see. Well, we'll certainly help you. I've never dealt with undines, but Tryg and Thor think they have everything in hand, and I trust them."

Mordred nodded curtly. "I trust them, too." He knew the reason he was freaking out was because Amyas wasn't here with him and that it had nothing to do with how he felt about Thor and Tryg. If it had been anyone else kept prisoner, he wouldn't have been acting this way. As it was, he couldn't stop himself from worrying and wanting Amyas back.

He forced himself to take a deep breath. He needed to be calm. He couldn't antagonize these allies, not when they were vital to this mission. "What do you have in mind, then?" he asked Thor.

"Tryg and I are draugr. We can shift into different animals, and that includes seals. I want to dream walk into Amyas's dreams to explain what's going on. He can give me all the details he has about where he's being kept, security, things like that. Once we have all the information, Tryg and I will swim into the lake and find him."

"I'm pretty sure the tribe will notice two seals swimming around. This isn't seal territory."

"You'd be surprised at what people notice and don't notice. Besides, we know what we're doing. Even when we're in our shifted forms, we're still us, which means we keep all the experience and training we have. I'm sure we can do this. We can also create bad weather, something that will distract the tribe while we're there. We're immune to weapons, so that won't be a problem. They would have to try hard to kill us, and I doubt they know how to do it. Besides, even if they knew, they wouldn't be able to. As you know, the only people who can kill us are heroes, and there are no heroes in the lake."

Mordred felt the need to lean back in his chair in relief. It was a good plan, even though he had no part in it. He wanted to be the one to save Amyas, but he couldn't, not this time. The job would go to Tryg and Thor, and even though it made Mordred nervous, he knew it was the best thing everyone could do right now. He trusted them, and he had to show that. "All right. When will you dream walk into Amyas's dreams?"

"The sooner we do this, the better it will be. I can do it tonight. Then tomorrow, we'll go get him. We could even do that during the night so fewer people will notice us. It will depend on what Amyas has to say about security and how many guards are around."

Relief gripped Mordred's chest. They were going to help Amyas, and they were going to do it soon, over the next few days. By the end of the week, he would have Amyas back, and this entire situation would be a bad memory.

"There's something else," Bayard said.

Everyone turned their attention to him. He stared at Mordred until Mordred realized what he wanted him to talk about.

Mordred cleared his throat. "The conclave contacted me. I'm still confused about this situation. I don't know what they thought they would obtain by calling me since they no doubt already know I wasn't going to stop."

"They actually asked you to stop?" Thor asked. He sounded incredulous.

Mordred understood that feeling. When he thought about the phone call, he still had no idea what had happened.

He might be able to understand the conclave asking him to stop, but Ceara had threatened him several times. Shouldn't she have tried to be friendly to him? Unless even though she'd asked him to stop, she'd already known he wouldn't. But then, why had she called? "They did. They also threatened me several times."

Tryg snorted. "No one's surprised by that."

"We can deal with the conclave once this thing with Amyas is over," Mordred declared. He wanted everyone in the room to focus on Amyas. "A few more days isn't going to change anything."

Or at least, he hoped so. He had enough trouble with Amyas right now. He didn't need the conclave to start poking at him. It would be exactly like them to do just that, though, which meant he had to warn his heroes before things got dicey.

Amyas was sleeping again. He didn't have anything else to do in the situation he was in, so he'd decided that resting would probably help. It meant he wasn't bored, but also that he wasn't in pain, which was what he needed.

Today was weird, though. Amyas knew he was sleeping, but the dream felt so real. He looked around, wondering where he was. Everything was foggy, but as he waited, he started seeing more details, and he recognized the house.

He was home, in the home he and Mordred shared.

Emotion gripped his throat. He wanted to go back. He wanted to be able to leave this place and never come back. He wanted to be where he belonged, with Mordred and their friends.

"Amyas," a tall man said.

Amyas had to squint to recognize him. "Thor. What are you doing in my dreams?" It didn't make sense. Amyas barely knew Thor, and if he was honest, he was kind of intimidated by the man. He knew what kind of creature Thor was, and while he was in awe, he was also kind of scared. Draugr weren't known for being friendly, even though so far, Thor hadn't done anything that had freaked Amyas out.

Thor smiled kindly. "I'm actually here to talk to you."

Amyas looked around again. Furniture had started to appear around them, and he recognized the living room. It looked ready for another movie night, which made his heart ache. He wanted all of that back. He wanted to go home, and he didn't understand why his parents and Necsa wouldn't allow him to. Was it so bad that his home wasn't with them anymore?

"Amyas," Thor said. "We need to talk, and we need to do it now."

"Why? You're a dream."

"I'm not."

"I'm pretty sure we're in my dreams, so yes, you are."

Thor huffed, but thankfully, he didn't look angry. "What do you know about draugr?"

"Is this a lesson on supernatural beings? Because I'd rather watch a movie."

"Dammit, I wished I'd gotten to know you better before you were kidnapped. It's not a lesson. I know you think this is all a dream, and it is, but it also isn't."

Amyas blinked. "That doesn't tell me anything."

"Draugr can walk in other people's dreams. We can manipulate them, and we can communicate through them. You're not imagining me. I'm actually here, and I need to talk to you. Mordred wants you to be rescued, and if that's what you want, too, we'll help you."

Amyas's heart raced in his chest. He wanted to reach out to Thor to see if he actually was real, but he was also afraid that his hand would go through him. "You're actually here?" he asked, keeping his hands to himself.

"I am. You have to tell me exactly where you are and how many guards are around. That way, Tryg and I can rescue you."

"You won't be able to. I'm in the water."

"You don't have to worry about that."

"It's kind of hard not to."

"Tryg and I can shift into seals. Now tell me everything I should know about the tribe and the people who live there. We're coming to get you, and we're going to do it soon."

Amyas still wasn't a hundred percent sure he wasn't dreaming, but in the off chance he actually wasn't, he couldn't miss this opportunity to get out of here. "What do you want to know exactly?" he asked.

"I need a rough idea of the village's layout and where you are. I assume you're still a prisoner?"

"They're keeping me in a cell."

"Okay. Can you draw me a map of the village and where you think bad weather would do the most damage? We're going to use it as a distraction."

Amyas didn't have anything to write on, but as he looked around, a piece of paper and a pen materialized out of nowhere. He supposed there were good sides to having this conversation in his dreams.

He quickly drew a map of the village, adding crosses where he knew bad weather would make the most damage. He felt kind of guilty knowing how much work the village would have to fix things, but he reminded himself that they were keeping him a prisoner for no reason. It helped, and as he and Thor continued talking about what the plan was, he started to get hopeful.

He hadn't been able to find a way to save himself, but maybe he didn't have to. Maybe Thor and Tryg would be enough, and he would soon be out of here. He couldn't wait to be with Mordred again and to be free. What Necsa and his parents were doing to him wasn't fair, and he hoped he never saw them again once this was over. He felt betrayed, and that was a hard feeling to get over.

"All right," Thor said as he grabbed the piece of paper and stuffed it in his pocket. Amyas wondered if it would disappear when he woke up. "I think I have everything I need."

"When are you coming?" Amyas needed to know. He wanted to be ready, but he also wanted the feeling of despair to leave his chest.

"Do you think this would be better to do during the night? Or are there more guards when everyone is sleeping?"

"I can't tell you how many guards are outside because I haven't been allowed out since I came back, but the village isn't big. We don't have a lot of tribe members, so if the bad weather causes problems, everyone would have to pitch in.

They'll leave me here because they'll think I can't get out of the cell anyway. Your best bet is probably to do it during the night when most people are sleeping. It'll take more time to get everyone on their feet and where they have to fix the damage, but they'll be distracted. You have to be careful, though. Necsa isn't a normal undine. She's our leader, and she's fierce. She won't hesitate to attack, unlike most other undines in the village."

"Mordred told us about her. What about the other tribe members? Do you think they're going to try to stop us from getting to you?"

"My parents might if they realize what's happening. I doubt anyone else would, though. We're not fighters. I don't even know what most of them think about me being a prisoner, but they won't stand up to you."

"That's all I needed to know. Be ready. Get some rest now that you have the chance to do so. You'll be back home soon, and you won't ever have to worry about this again." Thor started to fade, but Amyas needed him to know something first. "Thank you," he said.

Thor became more corporeal again. "What are you thanking me for? I'm doing what anyone would have done."

"Not really. My parents agree with Necsa that I needed to be kept here. They don't care about me, even though they're my parents. So thank you. You didn't have to do this, yet you're doing it."

"Well, Mordred is a friend, and you're important to him. I would do this and a lot more to help my friends."

"I never saw you at the house before."

Thor hesitated and looked around, but in the end, he gave Amyas an explanation. "Things aren't easy between Mordred and his people and the supernatural beings they're trying to help. That includes me. I was wary of Mordred in the beginning, and some days, when I remember what he was, I still am. He's not the man he was before, though, and I know that. He's a good person, and he deserves to be happy. If that means he needs you, I'm going to do everything I can to make sure he has you back. Besides, I don't think anyone should be held against their will or be forced to marry. Now get some real rest. Tryg and I will wait until it's dark to start the distraction. You need to be rested when we get to you."

Amyas nodded, but as soon as Thor was gone, he woke up. He couldn't help it, but as he opened his eyes, he smiled at the ceiling. He was getting out of here, and if he had a say in it, he was never coming back.

Mordred couldn't look away from Thor. Knowing that Thor was in Amyas's dreams talking to him was fascinating, and Mordred wanted to know more about how it worked. More importantly, though, he wanted to know how Amyas was.

He'd been wounded, but that was all Mordred knew. He had no idea what kind of wound Amyas had suffered or even where he'd been hit. Hopefully, it was nothing too bad, but there was no way for Mordred to know.

He pounced as soon as Thor opened his eyes. "How is he?"

Thor chuckled and moved into a sitting position. Cecil was there, gently touching his face and making sure he was okay. The two had a conversation with their gazes that Mordred couldn't understand, and he looked away. It felt too intimate for him to be staring at them while they were doing this.

"He's fine."

Mordred turned to look at Thor once again. "You talked to him?"

Thor nodded. He and Cecil were holding hands, but Thor looked okay, just like he had when he'd entered Amyas's dreams. "He was wounded, just like you said, but it's not as bad as I feared. He lost some blood, and he has stitches, but a healer took care of him, and he should be fine. He's in some pain."

"I'll have someone look at him as soon as he's here," Mordred promised.

"I have no doubt. But we talked about the plan, and he agreed that having a distraction was a good idea. He also told me to do it during the night so that everyone would be either too distracted by the bad weather or still trying to wake up. That means we only have a few hours to do this."

Mordred straightened. He'd been pacing while Thor was under, but he'd stopped when Thor had awakened. He started moving again, even though he knew Amyas was okay. "When are you going? Actually, when are *we* going?" He glared at Thor, silently daring him to suggest he stay here.

Thor raised his free hand. "I'm not going to tell you what you can or can't do. Besides, Tryg and I will need someone to portal us to the lake. It will be faster than any mode of transportation we can use. I suppose your second will want to come, too?"

Mordred looked at Bayard, who was sitting on the edge of an armchair. He wasn't going to ask, not if Bayard didn't want to come, but he was relieved when his friend nodded. Mordred turned his attention back to Thor. "He's coming, too. When are we going, then?"

"Give us a few hours."

Mordred huffed in irritation. "A few hours is too long. We don't have that kind of time."

"We're going to have to make that kind of time. I discussed it with Amyas, and he agrees that we should wait until most of the tribe is asleep. They don't have anything to fear in the lake, which means the warriors the leader trained will mostly be asleep. There will be a few guards, but that's it. Amyas was able to tell me exactly where he is, but he has no idea what kind of security we'll find outside of the cell. He hasn't been allowed out since he was put there. We have to be careful, Mordred."

Mordred understood that, but it didn't help. "Would you be careful if Cecil was the one who'd been kidnapped?"

Thor got to his feet, leaving Cecil on the couch. "I understand," he said, putting his hands on Mordred's shoulders.

Mordred was forced to look at him, and he didn't like it. He didn't want anyone to see him this vulnerable, least of all Thor, who in the end, was still an enemy.

No. That was wrong. That was Mordred thinking like he had when he'd worked for the conclave. Thor was a friend. He wouldn't be here if he wasn't, and Mordred had to focus on that. Both Thor and Tryg were helping him, and that was the only important thing.

"Besides, you have that meeting," Thor continued.

Mordred groaned. "I'm sure Eudocia can take care of it for me."

"She could, but she shouldn't have to. You're the leader here, not her, not Bayard. I understand you want to focus on Amyas, but there's nothing you can do right now. He's the center of your world, but other people depend on you. Do your job, and Tryg and I will do ours."

Mordred glared, even though Thor was right. "Fine. I'll have that meeting, and I'll explain everything that's happening."

"Good, because we're going to need more than you and Bayard to come with us to the lake. We have no idea what's going to happen once we free Amyas, and we might need backup. We also don't know if the conclave is a danger when it comes to the undines. They might find out we're there, and they wouldn't hesitate to strike. They're after Tryg and me as much as they're after you."

As much as Mordred wanted to go to the lake right now, he knew Thor was right. He had work to do, and he couldn't delegate.

He left Thor and Cecil in the living room and headed toward the big conference room he and his heroes used for crowded meetings. Everyone was there when he and Bayard arrived, and Mordred sucked in a breath.

Amyas wasn't his only responsibility, no matter how much he wished he was. Amyas would be angry at Mordred if he found out Mordred had neglected his mission and his people, and Mordred didn't want that to happen. This was as important to Amyas as it was to him and to all the people who were watching him right now. He had to focus on them and put his personal feelings to the side for at least half an hour.

"As I'm sure you already know, the conclave contacted me," he explained.

He noticed Tryg and Isaac sitting in a corner. Tryg was glaring at anyone who even dared look at Isaac, but Isaac was staring at Mordred, focused on what he was saying.

"They wanted me to surrender," Mordred continued. "I don't know whether or not they truly believe they're in the right, but they seemed to. They think we're hindering their mission, which is protecting humanity against all supernatural beings. They also threatened me, which I'm sure surprises none of you."

A few people in the room chuckled.

"What do you think they're going to do?" one of the heroes asked.

"I honestly have no idea. I have several contacts among the conclave heroes, and I hope they'll be able to find out before something actually happens. I'm sure the conclave at least suspects I have spies, though, so it's not going to be easy. They're going to try their hardest to get their hands on me, and on any of you. You have to be extremely careful from now on. Don't go anywhere alone if you can help it, and especially don't go on missions alone. Try not to get separated from your team. I'll organize another meeting as soon as I know more."

"I have a question," Isaac said, raising his hand. Mordred smiled at him. Isaac's cheeks were red, and he was obviously flustered, but he soldiered on. "How do you usually recruit heroes?" he asked.

This wasn't the question Mordred had expected. "I try talking to all the heroes we meet when we go on missions against the conclave."

Isaac frowned. "I can't imagine that works well."

"It doesn't, usually. Every time we capture a hero, we bring them back here. We lock them up, and we talk to them day after day until they understand." Or rather, until they saw the light. Mordred was working on Percival right now, although he wasn't putting much energy into it. He didn't have the time to focus on Percival, not with Amyas gone.

"That doesn't sound like the best way to do this. What you're saying is that the heroes still working with the conclave don't know what the conclave actually does," Isaac pointed out.

"I'm sure some suspect, but they prefer to look the other way."

Isaac shook his head. "You need to be more efficient. While you might be right that some no doubt look the other way, I'm sure that a lot of them would react differently if they knew what the conclave is actually doing. You need to let all of them know. Even if they suspect, it might give them the push they need. Look at what happened with Haven."

"Dimitri was the push he needed, not me and my people," Mordred pointed out.

"Maybe, but you're not telling the conclave heroes anything, so they can't make decisions. You have to find a way to let all of them know what's going on."

Mordred found himself agreeing, but now wasn't the time to do that. It was something he and the others needed to talk

about, and he wasn't going to be able to focus on that or anything else until Amyas was back home, safe and sound.

Chapter Thirteen

Mordred had expected Amyas and what was going on with him to keep him distracted for the rest of the evening, but he couldn't stop thinking about what Isaac had said. The meeting had broken up after that conversation, and they hadn't found a solution. There had to be one, though.

Isaac was right. Mordred was sure that if someone had told him what the conclave was doing and showed him how wrong it was, he would have left decades before he actually had. He'd been taught to respect the conclave and the decisions they made since the conclave had found him. They'd trained him, both physically and mentally, which was why it had taken him so long to see what they were doing. He knew the same went for all the heroes now working with him. None of them were proud of how long they'd managed to ignore how wrong the conclave was behaving.

Surely, the same had to go for the heroes still working with the conclave.

Mordred had come up with a plan, although he wasn't sure how realistic it was. He needed to talk to someone who knew more about computers than he did, and while his organization had someone, he decided to go straight to the source of the idea.

He found Isaac, Tryg, Thor, and the rest of their little group in the living room, talking. Isaac smiled when he noticed Mordred, and Mordred made a beeline for him, ignoring the glare Tryg sent his way. "I've been thinking about what you said during the meeting," he said, sitting next to Isaac.

Tryg looked like he wanted to tear Mordred's head clean off his shoulders. Isaac, on the other hand, was beaming. "You were? I wasn't sure it was a good idea."

"I think it's a great idea. You're right. If someone had told me what the conclave was doing, I would have left decades earlier than I actually did. Even when I had a niggle of doubt that something was going on, the conclave was all I knew, and they'd taught me well. It took me a long time to gather the courage to go against them, and even then, I just left. I didn't stand up for what I thought was right."

"It looks to me like you're doing that now, though."

"Maybe. But I want to find a way to tell all the heroes what's going on. Do you think it's something we could do through the conclave's computers?"

Isaac blinked, then grinned. "That's a great idea. You have no other way to get all the heroes' phone numbers or emails, right?"

"No, but I know that the conclave uses a program they built to keep in contact with all the heroes. It gives them their marching orders and their missions, things like that. It would be the perfect way to let all the heroes know what the conclave is up to."

"And it would use their technology against them. I like that."

"The problem is that I have no idea how to do that."

Isaac wrinkled his nose. "Well, I'm good with computers, but I'm not sure I can help. Don't you have computer people?"

"I do, and I thought you'd like to meet them."

Isaac looked like a kid in a toy store. "I can?"

Now probably wasn't the right moment to ask Isaac and everyone else to stay, but since Mordred was thinking about it, he looked around. Dimitri and Haven were already part of his rebel group, but Tryg and Isaac and Thor and Cecil weren't. "All of you are welcome to stay with us for as long as you want, and since you're here, I'd like to talk about something."

"The answer is no," Tryg said.

Thor rolled his eyes and hit him on the back of the head. "Listen to him, at least."

"I already know what he's going to say. He wants us to work with him. He wants us to work with *heroes*."

"You're right," Mordred agreed. "We *are* heroes. Nothing we can do or say will change that, because it's the way we were born, just like you were born a draugr and Isaac was born a human. You know what we do, though. You know we don't work for the conclave. We're trying to right the wrongs we did, and I could use your help."

"What's in it for me, though?"

"You would have allies. You don't have to live with us the way most former heroes do, but I'd like you to be part of our group. You would be safe here, and so would Isaac. He would be able to work with people who enjoy the same things he does. I can see how much you love him, but I think he needs other people in his life."

Mordred was pretty sure Tryg was about to pound him into the floor, but luckily for him, Isaac put a hand on Tryg's arm. That was enough to stop Tryg from doing whatever he'd been planning.

Isaac looked at Tryg, and Mordred felt like he was intruding on the private moment. "He's not wrong," Isaac murmured.

"I just want to protect you," Tryg answered.

"I know, and I love you for that, and for a lot of other reasons. But I enjoy spending time with Thor and Cecil, and Dimitri and Haven. I love you, but I was alone for so long. I think it's time for me to have more than just you in my life. It won't change how I feel about you, and I know we should talk about it before making decisions, but please, don't dismiss Mordred's offer just because he's a hero. You know what people think of you and Thor just because of what you were born as. Don't make the same mistake."

Mordred expected Tryg to say no anyway, so he was surprised when Tryg nodded curtly. "Fine. I'll consider it, and we'll talk," he told Isaac.

Isaac grinned and kissed Tryg. "Thank you." He turned to Mordred. "Do I get to meet your computer people, then?"

Mordred got to his feet. "We can go now."

They looked like a procession, the entire group walking down the hallways until they reached the computer room. Mordred didn't spend a lot of time there since he didn't understand much about computers, but he knew it was impressive, from Isaac's delighted expression. He wanted only the best for his people and the people they saved, and he'd spent a lot of money to set it up.

"Everyone, this is Isaac. He had the idea of using the conclave's computers to send a video message or an email to all the heroes who still work for them."

"I think a video message would be more impactful," Isaac said.

Mordred nodded at him before turning his attention back to the room. "He'd like to work with you when it comes to hacking the conclave's system and find a way to make this work. What I want to know is if you think it's doable."

Alger, the guy in charge, rolled his chair back from his desk and stood. He rubbed his face with his hands, then looked at Mordred. "It depends. It's not something we've attempted yet, but I worked with the conclave's computers when I was still with them. I'm sure I can find my way around them, but if they've changed anything since I left, it might not be possible. I can't make promises."

Mordred squeezed Alger's shoulder. "Do what you can

and let me know."

"You're going to get Amyas tonight?"

Mordred nodded. "I will. But tomorrow, he'll be home, and we'll be able to focus on this."

"Get him back. By the time you're done, I'll have an answer for you."

Mordred's chest felt tight. They truly were a family who cared about each other, and he couldn't believe it had taken Amyas for him to realize that. That was one of the reasons Amyas was so precious, not just to Mordred, but to everyone else.

He was part of their family, and they were getting him back.

Amyas jerked into an upright position when the door to his cell opened. Now that he knew Mordred was coming for him, he was afraid someone would find out and try to stop him. Amyas hoped it was his parents visiting him because they'd be harmless if something happened while they were here, but of course, it wasn't.

It was Necsa.

She stepped into the cell, and Amyas watched her. He didn't know why she was here. She had to be aware of the fact that he hadn't changed his mind yet. He had no doubt that his parents had talked to her, and while he was curious as to why she was visiting him, he also couldn't help but wonder if maybe she suspected Mordred was going to try to get to him.

"How is your arm?" Necsa asked.

Amyas swallowed. He had to relax before she realized something was going on. It wasn't time for Thor to come yet, and Necsa would be gone by the time it happened. "It's been better."

Necsa nodded. "Make sure to ask the healer if you need

more painkillers."

Necsa was being nice, which was suspicious. "Did something happen?" Amyas asked. His mind was racing as he tried to find an explanation for her behavior.

She stayed close to the door, watching him. "I suppose it depends on what you're asking exactly."

"You're being nice. You're still keeping me prisoner, and you told me I wouldn't be allowed out of the cell until I went along with what you want me to do, but you're asking me about my wound."

Necsa sighed. "I don't take pleasure in keeping you locked up."

Amyas snorted. It probably wasn't the best idea to antagonize Necsa, but he was still angry. "Could have fooled me."

Her eyes narrowed. "You can't be with a hero, Amyas. The only people you can be with is either a human so you'll get your soul, or with an undine."

"And who decides that?"

"It's always been like that."

"I don't care!" Amyas sucked in a breath. Yelling at Necsa would only make things worse. "I don't care if it's always been like this. I'm in love with Mordred, and I don't care that he's a hero. He and his people are trying to help us and other supernatural beings. He hasn't worked for the conclave in two hundred years, and he's never going back."

"But he can't change what he is."

"He can't," Amyas agreed. "Just like I can't change what I am. I also can't change how I feel, both about him and about everything else. Please, just let me go. I don't want anyone to get hurt."

Necsa frowned. "Why would anyone get hurt?"

"Do you really think I'm going to sit here and wait until you decide I'm brainwashed enough to be let out? Do you think you'll manage to convince me that the best thing for me is to marry a human? I'm an adult, and I don't want to be part of the tribe anymore. I haven't wanted it for a while, but I'd never had the opportunity to leave. I took it as soon as I did, and if I have another one, I'll take it, too."

"Seeing how much he brainwashed you is sad."

Amyas didn't know how to get through to Necsa. She was convinced that Mordred had done something to him to convince him to be with him, and it was kind of sad. "Have you ever loved someone?" he asked in a whisper.

She seemed nonplussed at the question. "I'm not sure it has anything to do with the conversation."

"It has everything to do with the conversation because if you'd ever loved someone the way I love Mordred, you would understand why I want to be with him."

"Undines don't marry for love. They marry to get a soul."

"Why would I want a soul? Are undines who don't find human beings to marry bad? Look at my parents. They love each other, they had two children, and they're part of this tribe. You don't have a soul, either, yet you're not running around looking for a human."

Necsa's expression hardened. "That's because I'm the leader. I had to sacrifice many things to take this role, but you can't understand."

"Just like you can't understand why I want to leave. I just want to be free to live my life the way I want to live it. Is that so bad?"

"I never had that opportunity," Necsa snapped. She pressed her lips together, which told Amyas she hadn't meant to say that.

He grabbed at the words, hoping they would help. "Because your father was our leader before you, and you had to take his place. You were raised knowing you would. And you're right—you had to give up a lot to become our leader. Why do you want to do that to me, too? You know how much it hurts. You know how angry it makes me. You've gone through this, and I don't understand why you'd wish it on someone else."

"The hero did a good job with you."

Amyas groaned in frustration. "Haven't you listened to anything I said? The hero didn't do anything to me. He gave me a home and the opportunity to decide what I wanted to do with my life. He didn't push me either way, not the way you are. Who do you think the bad guy is? The person who made me feel protected and safe enough to make my own decisions, or the person trying to force me into doing what they want?"

Necsa reached for the door. Amyas knew he'd lost her. He wasn't sure she'd listened to him anyway. He'd done his best, but she clearly wasn't going to change her mind.

She'd told him she had to make sacrifices to take her father's place, and she was asking him to do the same. He didn't have a reason to, though. He would never be the tribe leader. He didn't *want* to be the tribe leader, and he didn't even want to be part of the tribe.

"Are you going to keep me here for weeks?" he asked.

She paused with her hand against the door and turned her head to look at him. "If that's what it takes, yes."

"What if I never change my mind?"

"I hope you will. I can keep you in here for months, even for years. You'll stay a prisoner until you cooperate."

"And my jailers are the people who continue to say they love me and want what's best for me. You're not acting like you do." Amyas was bitter, but anyone would have been in his position.

He had come back to warn the tribe they were about to be attacked. He'd wanted to make sure everyone was okay and to help fight the conclave. How had the tribe thanked him? By locking him up and keeping him prisoner. By telling him that he was brainwashed and that what he had with Mordred wasn't real. He didn't care that they were doing it because they loved him and wanted the best for him. This wasn't the best, and he wouldn't allow anyone to change his mind about that.

"You'll realize, in time," Necsa said. "When you start forgetting what happened with the hero, you'll see that we did what we had to do. You're part of this tribe, Amyas, and you'll never leave it."

"You just said you wanted me to find a human to marry."

"I do, in time. But even when you do and have to stay on the surface, you'll still be a tribe member. This tribe is part of you. It's in your blood, and it will be in your soul when you gain one."

Amyas flopped back onto the bed. He'd done his best to convince both his parents and Necsa to let him go without a result. He wasn't going to try again. The only way for him to leave now was to wait for Thor to arrive. He didn't care what happened to the tribe and his parents once he was free. If they were attacked again, he wouldn't come back.

He'd wanted to help, and they'd betrayed him. It wasn't a wound that was going to heal anytime soon, and he found himself satisfied by the thought that when his parents came tomorrow morning to see him, they would find the cell empty, and they wouldn't know what had happened to him.

They would never find out. The thought that they would be clueless for the rest of their immortal lives made Amyas feel slightly guilty, but then his anger took over. They deserved this, while he didn't.

He deserved to be *free*, and he was going to be.

Mordred tried to breathe in and out, but it wasn't easy. His chest felt tight, and he briefly wondered if he was having a heart attack before remembering that he couldn't. It sure felt like he might be about to, though.

"Mordred?" Bayard asked from the open door of Mordred's office.

"It's time?" Mordred answered.

He'd wanted to hang in the living room with Thor and Tryg while he waited for the time to get Amyas, but he'd decided to go to his office instead. Everyone knew how eager he was to get Amyas back, but he didn't want to interrupt whatever Thor and Tryg needed to do before they left. They understood how nervous and anxious he was better than a lot of people, but that didn't mean they would take it nicely if he bothered them. The dream walking, the shifting, all of that had to be hard to do and energy-consuming. They needed space and time to get ready, which was what Mordred had done his best to give them.

He was more than ready to go get Amyas, though.

Bayard shook his head and stepped into the office. "You have a message from the conclave."

Mordred groaned. Now wasn't the moment for him to have to deal with the conclave. "What do they want?"

"You should see for yourself." He handed Mordred a tablet, and Mordred took it gingerly. He didn't want to do this now. He had other things to focus on, but of course, the conclave wouldn't care about that. They didn't even know about it.

He stared at the screen in front of him. He'd expected an email, but it was a video message, just like the one he was planning on sending to the heroes. He wasn't surprised to see Ceara on the screen. She looked how he remembered. Her expression was dark, angry, which wasn't a surprise coming from her, especially after the conversation they'd had on the phone. "Have you already watched it?" Mordred asked.

Bayard nodded curtly. "I did."

"Is it as bad as I think it is?"

Bayard's lips twisted into a smile. "It depends on what you mean by bad. It's not pleasant."

Mordred snorted. "When is anything pleasant when it comes to the conclave?"

"True. You should watch it. That way, you won't have to think about it while we're away rescuing Amyas."

Mordred wouldn't have worried about it. He should focus on Amyas and on making sure he was okay. Still, this was his job, and he needed to do it. He had to be sure the conclave wouldn't find the house and attack while he was gone. He doubted that was the case—they'd been trying to find him for two hundred years, and they hadn't yet managed. Nothing had changed, not so much that they would know where he was.

He sighed and pressed the play button.

"Mordred," Ceara started. She stared right at Mordred. "This message is to ask you to surrender. You and your people need to stop this. The conclave will welcome everyone who wants to come back, except for you. If you don't agree to this, we'll hunt and kill all of you." She paused. "Is that really what you want? The heroes working with you are your people. All the heroes are. Do you really want some of them to be killed by their brothers and sisters? Are you that cruel?"

Mordred blinked at the screen. He wasn't surprised at the tone of the message or even at what was being said. This was how the conclave operated.

"We can't welcome you back, but the others will always have a place with us. As for you, you will be put to death. I'm sure you expected this, and I can promise you we'll make it as painless as we can."

She didn't look happy about that, and Mordred suspected that she'd already volunteered to get rid of him. She truly was bitter about his leaving the conclave and taking some of the heroes with him.

"If you don't obey immediately, everyone will be killed. What you did is treason, and the conclave can't accept that. This is the last chance you'll be given. Either you and your people surrender, or you'll be hunted. We won't stop until we kill all of you, and we'll bring the peace back into this world."

She stared at Mordred for a while longer before reaching for something. The image disappeared, and the video stopped.

Mordred put the tablet down. "That was something," he said.

"I agree," Bayard answered. He sat in the chair on the other side of Mordred's desk. "I already know you won't surrender."

"I won't. I have to tell the others about this, though."

"No one will go back to the conclave, no matter how much they threaten us."

Mordred knew that. All the heroes who worked with him were convinced of what they were doing. Those who weren't had never been a part of their group. Even if given the opportunity, none of the people who worked with Mordred would go back to the conclave. That put them in mortal danger, though.

So far, they'd managed to fly under the radar. The conclave had focused on supernatural beings and had dismissed the fact that sometimes their heroes were defeated by other heroes. They weren't anymore. They had Mordred in their sights, and they wouldn't stop until they had what they wanted, which was him dead.

A knock on his open office door made him jerk. He looked up to see Thor staring, a frown on his face. "Everything okay?" Thor asked.

Mordred swallowed. "It's fine. Are you ready?"

"We are. Are you still sure you want to come with us? Because you look pale."

"I need to have a chat with Eudocia before we go, but I'll be right with you."

"You know we'll do everything we can to get Amyas back. You should stay here if something happened."

Mordred got to his feet, shaking his head. "Nothing happened yet. The conclave sent me a message. They want us to surrender. Apparently, they'll take back the heroes who left, but I'll be killed."

Thor arched a brow. "Did you expect anything different?"

"I'm surprised they would want the heroes who left back. I suppose they'd make an example out of them."

"Do they know about this place?"

"I'm positive they don't."

Thor nodded. "It can wait, then."

"It can, and it will. Right now, my main goal is to get Amyas back. Once I have him here, I can focus on the conclave and what my answer to their message will be." Mordred already had a few words in mind, and the conclave wouldn't like them. He was worried, but he managed to push all of that to the back of his mind. The house was safe, as were the heroes who lived there.

When he found Eudocia waiting for him and the others in the house entrance, he gave her the tablet so she could watch the message and told her to let all the heroes who worked with them know about it. They needed to be careful, and if at all possible, to stay in the house. It was well protected, with a security system made up both of human technology and supernatural means. The conclave wouldn't be able to get through, even if they found the place.

There was nothing else Mordred could do for now, and he trusted Eudocia to do the best for their people.

"Ready to go?" he asked, looking at the little group around him.

Thor, Tryg, Haven, Dimitri, and Cecil were coming, as was

Bayard. Isaac would be staying with the heroes, but he was in the entrance, hovering close to Tryg. They were quietly talking, and Mordred looked away.

"Open the portal," Thor said.

Mordred took a deep breath and obeyed.

Amyas had been afraid he wouldn't know when Thor would arrive, but he shouldn't have. He knew something was happening as soon as it started.

There was always a strange tension in the water when the weather was bad on the surface. Usually, it didn't impact the village. It only happened when the storm was particularly bad, which was about once or twice a year, if they were unlucky.

The storm was going to be a huge one.

Amyas pressed himself closer to the bars at the window to look outside. The village had been quiet until a few moments ago. Now, people were stepping out of their houses, looking around as if expecting the village to be gone. Amyas wouldn't have been surprised if that had happened. The tension in the water felt strong enough to eradicate the village and disperse the houses and the people who lived there.

Undines were calling out to each other, but Amyas couldn't see or hear much. He rushed to the door instead, knocking and hoping against all odds that he would be let out. "Is anyone there? I can help if you let me out," he yelled.

No one answered, and Amyas was pretty sure that whatever guard had been posted there—if there had been one, something he wasn't a hundred percent convinced of—was gone. Amyas was virtually alone while the village around him shook and its inhabitants tried to save what they could from the anger of the storm.

Amyas could do nothing but wait. He didn't like it, and he

didn't like the thought that the village might get hurt by the storm, but what alternative was there? Necsa wasn't going to allow him to go, and as far as he was concerned, even though the other tribe members weren't the ones keeping him prisoner, they were just as bad as his parents. No one had stood up for him. No one had tried to convince Necsa she was wrong. Amyas hoped everyone would make it out okay, but it wasn't his problem anymore.

His parents had made sure of that.

He moved to the window again, peeking out. When he looked toward the surface, he could see how angry the water was. It moved quickly, and if a human had been there, they would have drowned. Amyas couldn't remember seeing such a bad storm, and he was sure it was the work of Tryg and Thor.

He waited. He didn't know how much time passed before he heard movement at the door. He moved toward it, hoping Thor was here to get him out. He had no idea how Thor would do it. They'd talked about the plan, but it seemed outlandish to him, even though he hoped it would work.

Someone knocked. Amyas stepped back, but he didn't go far.

The door swung open. Amyas held his breath, briefly wondering if Necsa had found out what was happening and had decided to come to find him, but it wasn't her. Instead, two big gray seals swam into the cell.

For whatever reason, Amyas found the sight hilarious. He'd never seen a seal in real life. There were no seals in the lake, so he wasn't familiar with them. He knew these weren't normal seals, though, and he had to press his lips together so he wouldn't start laughing.

"Thor?" he asked.

One of the seals moved closer and brushed against him. Amyas supposed it meant this was Thor, and he answered by brushing his fingertips against Thor's side.

The other seal looked grumpy. It grunted, watching the door. Amyas knew it meant they had to hurry, and he was all for that.

"Show me the way," he said.

The grumpy seal went ahead, while Amyas stuck with Thor. They snuck out, and just like Amyas had suspected, the village was a mess. People were running around now, yelling at each other and asking for help. His heart squeezed with guilt, but he focused on what he was doing and why. He and the two seals managed to get to the edge of the village before someone noticed them. He didn't look back to see who called out for him. He couldn't afford to.

Instead, he continued swimming, grateful that he wasn't alone. Thor and Tryg didn't seem worried about whoever was behind them, and Amyas hoped it meant that the person had stayed back at the village. The problem was that he couldn't read the seals' expressions, so he might be wrong. They could be worried, for all he knew.

They reached the surface without a hitch. Amyas took a deep breath as soon as he was out of the water, grinning like a fool even though it was windy and raining. He wasn't home yet, but he'd escaped his cell, and even the pain in his arm wasn't enough for him to stop from smiling.

He looked up, and there was Mordred. He was waiting, but his gaze found Amyas as soon as Amyas was out of the lake. He took a step forward, and Amyas moved toward him. Thor and Tryg shifted next to him, transforming from seals to human beings, and Tryg turned toward the storm.

It stopped raining.

The shift and everything else were impressive and quirky, but Amyas didn't have the time to focus on them now. He reached for Mordred, who was wadding into the water to reach him.

A hand wrapped around his ankle and pulled.

Amyas stumbled back into the water. He turned around to see that Necsa was behind him, holding him and trying to pull him back down toward the village. He tried kicking her in the face—and he didn't even feel guilty about it—but she twisted and caught his second ankle.

"How dare you," she said.

"I just want to be free," Amyas cried out.

"You belong with us. Did you really think I would allow you to leave?"

Amyas wriggled, and when he couldn't free his legs, he reached out and grabbed Necsa's hair. It wasn't exactly what Eudocia had been training him to do, but it worked. He pulled, and Necsa yelped in surprise. She let go of one of his legs, and this time, when he kicked her in the face, his foot made contact. Necsa let go of him completely, and he scrambled to his feet, trying to get away from her.

His back hit something hard and warm arms wrapped around him. He would have recognized them anywhere, and he instantly relaxed.

"You will pay for this," Necsa spat out. Her nose was bleeding.

"You know what my friends and I are capable of," Mordred said. "You lost. Accept it and let Amyas go without fighting us."

Necsa pointed a finger at Amyas, ignoring Mordred. "You dishonor the tribe. You will pay for it. I was willing to let you live with us, but now, you have to die. I won't allow you to make people think I'm a weak leader."

She moved fast, too fast for Amyas to react. One second, she was reaching for her side. The next, she had a knife in her hand and was rushing toward Amyas.

Mordred twisted them around so his back would be to Necsa. Amyas cried out. He didn't want Mordred to be hurt, least of all to rescue him. Amyas tried to turn them around again, but Mordred was too big and strong.

"Stay still," Mordred said.

"She's going to kill you," Amyas protested.

Right then, they both realized that nothing was happening. Necsa should already have reached them, but she hadn't, and it didn't make sense.

Amyas wriggled until Mordred loosened his hold on him. Once he could, he looked around him and sucked in a breath. Necsa was lying in the water, blood spreading around her. Her eyes were open and she was staring at the sky, but she wasn't seeing anything.

She was dead.

The knife she'd been about to use against Mordred was stuck in her chest. Amyas had no idea what had happened, and he looked around for an explanation. Thor and Tryg were still standing in the water, and they were both watching Necsa's body.

"What happened?" Mordred asked.

Thor rubbed the back of his neck. "Sorry about that. When I tried to stop her from stabbing you, she didn't take it well."

"And you killed her?"

Thor's expression shifted. "It was either that or let her kill you, and I wasn't about to let that happen."

CHAPTER FOURTEEN

Mordred couldn't look away from Necsa's body. He was used to fighting people and death, but this was entirely different. He understood Thor had done what he had to in order to protect both himself and Mordred and Amyas, but he was terrified that Amyas would blame him for this.

He wouldn't be wrong if he did.

None of this would have happened if Mordred hadn't allowed Necsa and the warriors to capture him. It wouldn't have happened if he'd waited for his people to get to him instead of allowing Amyas to free him. It wouldn't have happened if he had left Amyas behind when he'd run away after Amyas had freed him.

Necsa's death rested on Mordred's shoulders, and he had no idea what to do or to say. He wanted to apologize, to beg Amyas to forgive him, but he couldn't even seem to get a word out of his mouth.

The water gurgled, and a warrior appeared. Mordred took a step back, taking Amyas with him, but that was the only thing he could do. He would deserve to be captured and killed. He was the reason Amyas's tribe had lost their leader, and who knew what would happen to them now?

"That's it," someone snapped behind Mordred. "We have to go, and we have to do it now. If he's not going to do it, I will."

Mordred blinked and looked to see Haven and Bayard both opening a portal. Haven shoved his friends through it while Bayard focused on Mordred. "We have to go," he said, his gaze fixed on the warriors behind Mordred and Amyas.

"We should apologize," Mordred found himself saying. It was probably the stupidest thing he'd ever said.

Bayard looked at him like he was crazy. "Are you serious? Because they're not going to listen to you. They're going to kill you and Amyas, and they'll feel justified doing it."

"They would be. We killed their leader."

"Because she tried to kill you and Amyas." Bayard grabbed Mordred's hand and pulled. "Let's go. Do it for Amyas. He deserves to have a free life and to be safe."

That finally got Mordred into motion. He'd known he was acting like an idiot the entire time, but thinking about Amyas's safety was enough to make him grab his boyfriend, haul him off his feet, and rush to the portal.

They could talk about this later. If Amyas decided he couldn't be with Mordred anymore because of what Mordred had caused, Mordred would let him go. First, he had to keep him safe.

"Amyas!" a woman screamed.

"Mom?" Amyas answered.

It broke Mordred's heart, and he paused, forcing Bayard to stop, too.

"What have you done?" The woman sounded desperate.

"She tried to kill me," Amyas yelled.

"That's not possible. She wouldn't do something like that."

They didn't have time for this, but Mordred suspected this was the last time Amyas would see his parents, and he didn't want to take it away from him. He ignored Bayard, who was still trying to pull him along, and focused on Amyas.

"She wasn't a good leader. She imprisoned me and wouldn't listen to me. She tried to kill me, and I had to defend myself," Amyas explained.

Amyas's mother looked horrified. "You killed her?"

"Does it matter? She's dead, and you're going to have to

find a new leader. I'm sorry."

Amyas took a step closer to the portal. He and Mordred were holding hands now, and Mordred moved with him, ignoring Bayard's muttered, "Finally."

"Things could have been different," Amyas said. "If only you'd listened to me. I'm sorry this had to happen."

Then Amyas turned around and stepped through the portal. Mordred went along, more than happy to leave the situation behind. It wasn't over by a long shot, and Mordred would make sure the tribe had help if they needed it, but there was nothing else he could do. If he stayed, things would probably get worse, which was the last thing everyone needed.

The portal closed behind them. "That was close," Bayard said. He was staring at Mordred.

Mordred couldn't look at him. He couldn't look at anyone. How had this mission gone so wrong? Mordred understood that Necsa had died because she'd tried to kill Amyas, and in any normal circumstances, he would be sorry but not horrified. He couldn't stop thinking that Amyas was going to blame him for what had happened, though. That was why he couldn't look at his boyfriend. He was terrified of what he would see in Amyas's eyes, and he couldn't face it.

They couldn't stay in front of the house for the entire night, though. "We should go inside," he said, still not looking at Amyas. "Bayard, why don't you take Amyas to the infirmary? I want his arm to be looked at."

Bayard's eyebrows shot up. "Shouldn't you be the one going with him?"

"Later. I have things to do."

From the way Bayard was looking at him, Mordred knew he thought he was an asshole. He didn't care. He couldn't face Amyas's rejection right now. Eventually, he would be able to, but he needed a moment to breathe.

Now that Amyas wasn't looking at him, Mordred could

watch him as he walked inside the house, following Bayard. Was this the last time he'd have the opportunity to watch Amyas this way? Was Amyas going to demand to leave as soon as the healer was done with him?

"You're a dick," Haven said.

Mordred scowled at him. "Nothing changed, then."

Haven shook his head. "I don't get you. You have the man you love back, and you can't even look at him. What the fuck happened?" He didn't wait for an answer, walking toward the house instead. Mordred wondered if he and Dimitri would end up leaving, too.

He wouldn't be surprised if that was the case.

"Don't do that," Thor said.

"What are you talking about?" Mordred needed to go inside and face the music, both when it came to Amyas and the conclave.

"Don't push him away. How you feel doesn't matter. Amyas needs you, and you're not here for him."

"How can he need me after what just happened?"

Thor arched a brow. "Did you miss the fact that *I* was the one who killed Necsa? You had nothing to do with it."

"But she wouldn't have died if I'd done things differently."

Thor barked out a laugh. "If you could have seen the future, maybe. But even though I killed her, it was *her* fault. She shouldn't have imprisoned Amyas for wanting to live his life. She shouldn't have come after him and tried to kill him. Would you have wanted me to let her do that? She would still be alive then, but Amyas wouldn't be."

"We could have restrained her. We could have found another way."

"Maybe, maybe not. I don't feel guilty about killing her, and you shouldn't, either. *I* made that decision. If Amyas decides to hold you responsible anyway and leaves, then let him do that. But right now, he needs you, and you're not there for him. Let *him* decide how he feels about you and what happened. He left his tribe because no one would allow him to make his own decisions. Don't make the same mistake."

Mordred swallowed and looked at the house again. "You think he can forgive me for the role I played in Necsa's death?"

"I think you won't know until you talk to him. Probably not tonight. Give him some time to rest and wrap his mind around everything that happened. He's a smart guy, though."

"How do you know that? You barely talked to him."

"But I did, and I like him. It's obvious he loves you. I don't think this will change anything, but you should try to work things out together if it does. Don't shut him out, even though it's your first instinct. You're not alone in this, and he has as much right to his feelings as you do to yours. Ask him what he wants. Don't make the decision for him."

Thor was right. Mordred had been so focused on his own misery that he'd done what Amyas hadn't wanted anyone to do for him. He'd decided Amyas wouldn't want to see him or talk to him, and he'd kept his distance. Amyas had to be hurt and confused, and Mordred didn't want that.

He was going to have to apologize and maybe grovel. He was more than ready to do both those things, especially if they kept Amyas in his life.

Amyas was in shock. He couldn't seem to wrap his mind around what had happened, no matter how many times he thought about it.

Necsa was dead. She'd died because she'd tried to kill him.

Amyas didn't understand what he'd done to make her so angry. He'd gone against her orders, sure, but did that warrant death? He hadn't thought so. It had never occurred to him that she might react that way. He didn't understand.

Then there was the fact that his parents thought he'd killed her. Had they actually encouraged Necsa to kill him if he didn't do what they wanted? Amyas didn't want to think about that or to believe they would do something so horrible, but at this point, he wasn't sure about anything anymore. He hadn't thought they would agree with him being in jail because he didn't want to obey their orders, yet that was what they'd done.

"Are you okay?" Bayard asked as they walked toward the infirmary.

"I don't know. Physically, I'm fine, even though my arm hurts."

Bayard nodded. "But mentally and emotionally, it's different."

"It is. I can't believe she tried to kill me. I never did anything to her. I just wanted to live my life."

"And she should have allowed you to do it. What she did wasn't fair, and while I'm sorry she died, I'm not sorry that Thor killed her to protect you."

So it had been Thor. Amyas would have to thank him for saving his life. Mordred had been trying, too, and he would probably have succeeded, but he would have gotten hurt in the process, and Amyas couldn't even start to think about that. He didn't want anyone to get hurt because of him, least of all Mordred. Mordred had come for him when it would have been so much easier to leave Amyas in the lake. Mordred loved him, but he had more important things to worry about, and Amyas wouldn't have blamed him.

"I'm not sorry, either," Amyas murmured. "I never wanted things to go this way, but it was Necsa's fault, not mine, nor Thor's. I should thank him."

"Right now, you should see a healer and rest. You can talk to Thor and everyone else tomorrow morning."

They finally got to the infirmary, and Amyas stepped

inside. He wasn't surprised to see the healer was already there. She smiled at him. "How are you feeling?"

"I'm not sure. My arm hurts, but it's not what hurts the most."

She frowned. "What else?"

Thankfully, Bayard took her to the side to explain what had happened. Amyas didn't think he could have done it.

He sat on one of the beds and looked at the door. He hadn't missed the fact that Mordred wasn't with him. He understood Mordred had other things to focus on, but he couldn't help but feel hurt at the fact that Bayard was the one who was with him right now.

Did Mordred blame Amyas for Necsa's death? That was the thing that made the most sense. He'd been there, so he obviously wanted to help rescue Amyas, but things had gone horribly wrong. They wouldn't have if Amyas had been faster or if he'd been able to free himself instead of having to wait for Thor and Tryg to arrive.

"Do you want me to stay with you?" Bayard asked.

Amyas shook his head. "You should go to bed. I'll be fine. Vesta will take care of me."

"I promise I will," the healer confirmed.

Bayard didn't look convinced, but he went, leaving Vesta and Amyas alone. She checked Amyas's arm, cleaned the wound, and bandaged it again before declaring him healthy. Mordred still wasn't there once she was done, and it was obvious she wasn't sure what to do now.

"You can spend the night here if you feel more comfortable," she offered.

Amyas didn't know how to answer. Mordred was busy talking to Thor and the others, no doubt going over the mission and what had gone wrong. Should Amyas stay in the infirmary, or should he head to Mordred's bedroom?

He didn't like feeling insecure. He didn't usually feel like this, especially not when it came to Mordred. He knew Mordred loved him, and he loved Mordred. Whatever was going on, he should act normally. He had to be strong.

"I'll stay here for a bit longer if that's okay," he said.

"Of course. Do you want me to stay with you?"

"You should go to bed, too. I'm sorry you had to stay up so late."

She gently squeezed Amyas's forearm. "I wouldn't have had it any other way. You needed me, and I was happy to help. I'll check your wound again tomorrow, okay?"

Amyas nodded. She didn't linger, leaving him alone in the brightly lit infirmary. His head spun, and he was tempted to lie down and go to sleep. He wanted to see Mordred first, though, so he waited, hoping Mordred would come.

He almost cried out in relief when the door opened and Mordred stepped in. He looked around, frowning. "Where's Vesta? She was supposed to stay here and help you."

"She already did. She said the wound looks fine, although she wants to check it again tomorrow. I told her to go to bed."

"You should have done the same." Mordred stepped closer to the bed, stopping in front of Amyas. "You look tired."

Amyas swallowed. "I am. I was waiting for you."

Mordred grimaced. "I should have come sooner."

"The important thing is that you're here." Amyas leaned forward, and Mordred wrapped his arms around him. It felt like coming home, and Amyas closed his eyes. They burned with tears, but he wasn't sure why he was crying. Was it because Necsa was dead or because of how things had gone? Or maybe because he was finally home, and he was never leaving again?

"I'm sorry I left you alone. I shouldn't have," Mordred murmured.

"We can talk about it tomorrow. I know Necsa's death was my fault, but —"

"It wasn't, and I don't want you to think it was. She tried to kill you."

"Is Thor okay?"

"He's fine. He's not even sorry for what happened. He was only thinking about saving you, and he's convinced it's her own fault she's dead."

It made sense. Thor and Mordred had more experience when it came to death than Amyas ever wanted. It *was* Necsa's fault. She shouldn't have imprisoned him, and she shouldn't have tried to kill him. It was her decisions that had led to her death, so why did Amyas feel guilty?

Mordred sighed. "We should go to bed. Do you want to sleep here?"

Amyas shook his head. "I want to sleep in our bed. It's only been a few days, but I missed it." He tilted his head up to look at Mordred. "I missed *you*."

Mordred gently cupped one of Amyas's cheeks, still holding him with his other arm. "I missed you, too. I was used to sleeping alone, but now that I had to do it again, it wasn't possible. The bed was too empty without you in it."

"I never want to leave again."

Mordred kissed Amyas's forehead. "You don't have to. Whatever happens, whatever you decide, this will always be your home. If you decide you never want to leave the property, that's fine with me."

That was enough to give Amyas peace. He knew that by tomorrow, he would feel guilty again, but for now, this was enough. He was home with his family and the man he loved. He would be able to sleep tonight, and tomorrow, when he woke up, he would still be here. Eventually, he would be happy again, and he would be able to forget Necsa, and maybe even to forgive her.

CHAPTER FIFTEEN

When Amyas opened his eyes, he smiled at the ceiling. He wasn't in a cell anymore. He wasn't in the lake. There was no sign of water around him, and for once, he couldn't have been happier.

That was until he rolled to the side to look at Mordred and found the other side of the bed empty.

Amyas frowned and reached for Mordred's pillow. It was cold, which meant Mordred had gotten up a while ago. Why hadn't he stayed with Amyas?

Amyas tried telling himself it was normal. Mordred had been focused on getting him back for the past several days, and he'd no doubt neglected his work to do that. That meant he was doing some damage control right now, and maybe even reaching out to the tribe. Amyas wouldn't be surprised if he wanted to make sure the tribe was okay after losing their leader, even though Amyas himself wasn't about to contact his parents.

They were his past. Mordred was his future, and Amyas was now more than ever convinced he'd made the right choice, even though the consequences had been dire.

He took his time getting up and getting ready for the day. When he looked at the time, he realized how late it was. Now it made even more sense for Mordred not to be in bed with him. It was almost time for lunch, and Amyas never slept this late. He supposed he'd needed it. He hadn't slept well when he'd been locked up in his cell, and he needed to recuperate. He felt better, even though his arm was sore — and so was his heart.

Instead of going downstairs to get something to eat, he went looking for Mordred. He knew he was safe now, but he needed to set his eyes on Mordred and reassure himself. He didn't like feeling needy, but he knew Mordred would humor him and make sure he was fine.

The office door was closed, and Amyas knocked. He smiled when Mordred called out for him to enter and opened the door. "Good morning. You weren't in bed when I woke up," he said, stepping in.

Mordred barely looked at him. "I had things to do. It was late, and I can't afford to stay in bed until lunchtime."

Amyas frowned. "I know. I'm not angry at you for leaving."

"Good, because I have more work to do. While you were away, the conclave contacted us and gave us a deadline."

Amyas's stomach churned. "What kind of deadline?"

"They're demanding every single hero give themself up. They'll all be welcomed back into the conclave's ranks while I'll be executed. If they don't surrender, we'll *all* be killed."

"That's horrible. You're not thinking about doing what they're asking, are you?"

"Of course not." Mordred leaned back in his chair. "And I've already talked to Eudocia and Bayard. They agree with me. That doesn't mean we're not trying to do damage control. I need to be sure the conclave can't find this place and that if they do, the security system will keep them out. I'm sorry I don't have time for you."

"Of course. I understand." And Amyas truly did, even though he was hurt.

Mordred had always been loving, and he'd always had time for Amyas. More often than not, he didn't mind taking a break from his work or delegating to Bayard or Eudocia to spend time with Amyas. He'd barely looked at Amyas, though. It reminded Amyas of the way Mordred had acted last night, and it made him want to throw up.

"I guess I should go, then," he murmured.

Mordred's gaze was focused on his computer. "I'll find you later."

"All right." Amyas moved toward the door, hoping Mordred would stop him.

He didn't. Amyas stepped into the hallway and closed the door behind himself, leaning against it and wondering what had just happened.

Did Mordred regret saving him? Amyas wanted an answer to that question. He wanted to know if he was still welcome here. He didn't know who else to ask, though. Mordred wasn't going to talk to him, and he knew better than to push. Mordred had an excellent reason not to focus on Amyas right now, and maybe Amyas was just seeing things.

His stomach grumbled. He looked down, grimacing. He didn't want to eat, not after the conversation he'd had with Mordred, but he should. He'd been fed while the tribe had kept him prisoner, but he hadn't eaten much, and he felt kind of weak.

He headed to the kitchen, still thinking about how Mordred had reacted. He wasn't surprised to find that the kitchen wasn't empty. It never was, not with so many people living in the house. He recognized Cecil, even though they'd never really had time to talk, but he didn't know the second man.

Cecil smiled when he noticed Amyas. "Good morning. It's good to see you up."

Amyas forced himself to smile, but he wasn't sure the result was good. "Good morning. I guess that being kept a prisoner by your family makes you tired."

"There's food if you want. Oh, and this is Isaac. He's Tryg's boyfriend. Isaac, this is Amyas."

Isaac gave Amyas a wave, and Amyas couldn't help but

smile—for real this time. "It's a pleasure to meet you. I know you and Tryg came here to help, and I thank you for that."

"Don't. You needed help, and we were more than happy to provide it."

By the time Amyas settled at the counter, Cecil had already filled a plate for him. The smell of bacon and toasted bread hit Amyas's nose, and while his stomach grumbled again, he stared down at the plate, unable to eat. He felt nauseous at the thought that Mordred might decide he didn't want to be with him anymore.

What would he do if that was the case? Last night, Mordred had said that Amyas would always be welcome in this house and with these people, and Amyas knew that was true. But could he stay if he and Mordred weren't together? Could he stay away from Mordred, watch him day after day, and possibly finding someone else?

Mordred was Amyas's first love, and he'd thought he would be the last. Now, he wasn't so sure anymore, and he didn't know what to do with all of this.

"Is everything okay?" Cecil asked. He sounded hesitant, but when Amyas looked at him, he was staring.

Amyas shrugged. "I have no idea."

"We don't know each other well, but we can listen if you need to talk."

Amyas hadn't intended to talk to anyone. Dimitri was his closest friend, so maybe he would have mentioned something to him, but he felt guilty about everyone needing to rescue him. For whatever reason, though, his mouth opened, and everything tumbled out. "I'm afraid Mordred regrets saving me. He didn't come with me to the infirmary last night, and this morning, he wasn't in bed when I woke up. I went to his office, and he dismissed me without even looking at me. He didn't ask if I was feeling okay. He just told me he had work to do and that he had to focus on that. I understand, and I want everyone here to be safe, but it hurts."

Cecil and Isaac stayed silent as Amyas explained everything. He could see Cecil was angry, while Isaac was frowning. He didn't know what that meant, and once he was done, he snapped his mouth shut and waited.

"I don't think Mordred regrets saving you," Cecil said slowly. "He clearly loves you very much. You should have seen him when you were in the lake. He was going crazy, and he yelled at Thor and Tryg a few times because they weren't working fast enough."

"I agree," Isaac said. "Mordred loves you, even though he's behaving like an asshole."

"Maybe he feels guilty," Cecil pointed out.

Amyas frowned. "What are you talking about?"

"Well, even though I don't know him, I know Thor. If I were captured, he would feel guilty about one, allowing it, and two, in this situation, about Necsa getting killed."

Amyas blinked. "Why should he feel guilty about any of it? I willingly went into the lake, and even *I* didn't expect my parents and Necsa to imprison me. How could Mordred have? He barely knew them. And as for Necsa's death, she was the one who caused it. She tried to kill me, and even though Mordred would have killed her if he'd had to, he wasn't even the one who did that."

Cecil reached out and gently patted Amyas's hands. "Feelings aren't rational. He probably knows he had nothing to do with Necsa's death, but it doesn't mean he doesn't feel guilty. My advice is to talk to him."

Amyas snorted. "It's not going to be easy if he barely even looks at me."

Cecil arched a brow. "Are you going to let that stop you?"

Amyas stared at him for a moment. Cecil was right. Amyas wasn't going to let anything stop him from being happy, not even Mordred himself. He would get answers, no matter how hard Mordred tried to push him away.

Mordred always felt lost when he was in the computer room, but he had to leave his office. He was terrified that Amyas would come back to talk to him and he wouldn't know how to answer. This morning has been bad enough.

He'd desperately wanted to look at Amyas, but he'd been afraid of what he'd see if he did. He'd known better than to leave Amyas alone in bed, and he wouldn't have if the situation had been different. It wasn't, though, and he couldn't bear the thought of Amyas thinking he was the cause of Necsa's death, even though he was.

The whole situation was a mess, and Mordred wasn't sure how to deal with it. So he'd done the only thing he *did* know how to do, which was bury himself in his work. It wasn't working as well as he'd hoped, but he was sure that if he continued, it would.

It had to.

"So we managed to hack into the council's computers. The security system is good, but it's still the same as it was when I left, which isn't the smartest idea," Alger said.

Mordred had to focus on what the man was saying before he made a fool of himself. "You helped design it, didn't you?" he asked. He vaguely remembered something like that.

Alger grinned. "I did. It took a lot of work, and while it was stupid for the conclave not to change it, I'm happy they didn't. I'm even happier I'll be able to use it against them."

"Did you manage to find a way to contact all the heroes at once, then?"

"I did. I found the directory, and all the heroes are listed there, along with several ways to contact them. I should have thought about this sooner. I don't know why I didn't. The directory not only gives me access to all the heroes, but it also tells me the messages sent to them, including the missions. I know everything the conclave is doing now."

"I wish we'd thought about it sooner, too, but we didn't, and we shouldn't focus on that. Besides, we won't be able to use this for long. As soon as we broadcast whatever message I put together, the conclave will realize what's happening, and they'll put an end to it."

Alger pouted. "I know. It would have been so much easier to fight the conclave if we'd done this sooner."

"Don't worry about it," Mordred said, patting Alger's shoulder. "You're doing a great job, and I don't know where I would be if you weren't on my side."

Alger shrugged. "Probably drifting around with no friends."

Mordred laughed. Alger wasn't wrong. If Mordred didn't have the other heroes with him, he would be a loner. He'd always been, but then that was what most heroes were like. The conclave encouraged them to work on their own, unlike Mordred. It had taken him a while to realize that, but once he had, he'd thought it was because the conclave didn't want the heroes to talk to each other. It would make it easier for them to realize what was going on if they compared their experiences, which of course, was the last thing the conclave wanted.

"So now that I have a way to do this, what are *you* going to do?" Alger asked.

Mordred had to force himself to go back to the conversation. "Well, I need to decide what I'll say in the message. Everyone agrees it'll be a good idea to do a video, which I'm not thrilled about."

Alger grinned. "I bet you're not. You're going to do it, though, right?"

"I am. This is the best way we have to defeat the conclave."

Alger didn't look convinced. "Do you really think most

heroes will come to our side once we tell them about this?"

"Most? I don't know. A lot, I hope. We can't be the only ones thinking the conclave is wrong when they attack supernatural beings who did nothing wrong. Even if we don't manage to get all the heroes on our side, we'll get some of them, and it'll have to be enough, at least for now. Besides, if we tell the heroes about this, our truth will be out there. They'll be able to make their own decision about the conclave and what they do. It's all we can do. Every hero will have to deal with their own conscience and decide what they're willing to sacrifice to continue working for the conclave."

"What now, then?" Alger asked.

"Now, we're going to have a meeting. I want everyone to agree on this. I know Eudocia already talked to you about the threats I got yesterday, but I need to do that myself and to let everyone know what we're planning." And Mordred needed to know if any of his heroes were going to go back to the conclave.

Luckily, since Mordred had been worried about the conclave trying to attack his heroes, everyone was home, even the ones who didn't live there. It made it easy to get all of them to the big conference room with only a message, and when twenty minutes later he walked inside, they all turned to look at him.

Mordred had never liked this kind of meeting where everyone stared, but there was no way out of it.

"You all know about the threats," he started.

"And none of us are willing to surrender," Bayard intervened.

Mordred glared at him. "I'm aware *you* won't, but it doesn't mean no one here wants to." He looked around the room. "I'll understand if you decide to go back to the conclave. They're powerful, and they have more heroes than we do. We've always known our mission was dangerous, and if it's too dangerous for you, I won't try to stop you. You could go back to the conclave or leave and never look back. Whatever you feel more comfortable with, you should do it."

Mordred expected at least a few heroes to get up and leave, so he was surprised when no one did. He swallowed. His throat felt tight with emotion, and he had to clear his throat before he could continue. "All right. You know that my office door is always open if you want to talk about anything, including this. As to what our plans are now that the conclave revealed what *they* are planning, Alger managed to hack into their system. We have the names and contacts of every single hero with the conclave. I'm going to contact them through a video message and explain what the conclave has been doing and what they've been using the heroes for. Hopefully, at least some heroes will finally realize what's happening, and they'll come to our side."

"And if they don't?" someone asked.

"Then we'll have to hope that some will leave the conclave and disappear. The conclave can't touch us as long as we stay inside this house, but eventually, we'll have to leave. I want the conclave to be incapacitated as much as possible, whether it means we get their heroes or not."

There was nothing else to say, and Mordred declared the meeting over. He turned toward the door to leave and found Amyas blocking his way.

Amyas looked good, albeit tired. He'd had a good night's sleep, but it was going to take more than that for him to go back to how he'd been before. It wasn't just physical, either. Mordred suspected the betrayal weighed heavily on Amyas's shoulder, and he knew he should be doing more to help him carry that weight and come to terms with it.

Luckily for Mordred, Eudocia came up to Amyas to ask him how he was feeling. Amyas was distracted just long enough for Mordred to sneak out of the room. Mordred's heart was racing. He didn't even know why he was acting like this.

Or maybe he did. Last night, he'd promised Amyas he would always be there for him, and it wasn't a lie. He was terrified of what Amyas would say if he faced him, though. Because of Mordred's actions, Necsa was dead, and Amyas had lost his parents and tribe. Could he really not find Mordred guilty?

Mordred had promised himself he wouldn't make decisions for Amyas, but that didn't mean he wasn't terrified of knowing what those decisions would be. They needed to talk, but Mordred wasn't ready, and he wasn't sure he ever would be. Eventually, he would have to face Amyas, and for the first time since they'd met, the thought filled him with dread.

Amyas was waiting in Mordred's office. He felt ready to tear into Mordred, and he would make sure Mordred knew what he thought about the fact he was avoiding him.

Amyas was sure about that by now. He'd tried talking to Mordred after the meeting, but Eudocia had asked him how he was feeling, and he hadn't been able to avoid her. By the time they were done talking, Mordred had disappeared, which made Amyas even angrier.

Did Mordred really believe he could avoid Amyas forever? Was that what he was planning to do? Amyas wanted to know why, and he wanted to yell at Mordred for abandoning him when he needed him the most. To do that, he would have to manage to get to Mordred, though. It wasn't going to be easy if Mordred continued avoiding him, but he'd have to go back to his office eventually, right?

Amyas wasn't sure how long he'd waited, but he was ready to wait a lot longer to get his hands on Mordred.

When the door opened, he grinned. He was sitting on the

couch in the corner, and Mordred didn't notice him right away. Amyas took some time to look at the man he loved, and he felt a twinge of something in his chest.

Mordred had come to save him, even though it would have been much easier for him just to leave Amyas in the lake. That had to mean he loved Amyas, but it didn't explain why he was behaving the way he was now. Amyas had hope, though. This was just a misunderstanding, and they would deal with it and be happy together again. He didn't want to consider any other outcome.

Mordred closed the office door behind himself and headed toward his desk. Amyas stayed right where he was, and when Mordred finally noticed him, he arched a brow.

"What are you doing in here?" Mordred asked.

"I was waiting for you."

"I have work to do," Mordred said, gesturing toward his desk.

"I know, and I don't care."

Mordred's eyes widened, and he took a step back. "I'm sorry?"

Amyas got to his feet. "As you should be. I can't believe you're doing this."

"What are you talking about?"

Amyas came to stand in front of Mordred. Amyas wouldn't allow him to treat him the way his parents had. He was an adult, and he was able to decide how we want to live his life. "This avoiding me thing is bullshit," he said.

"What are you talking about?"

"Don't treat me like a child and like I don't know what I'm saying. I understand why you've been avoiding me. A lot happened, and it would have been easier for you to leave me with the tribe. Yesterday, though, you promised I would always be welcome here and that I'll always have a home with you. Today, you're acting as if I don't even exist. Either talk to me, or tell me you don't want me, and I'll go." Amyas had no intention of doing that, but Mordred didn't need to know that right now.

"Of course I want you. I'll always want you," Mordred murmured.

Amyas stood taller now that he had this certainty. "Then *talk* to me. Cecil seems to think you feel guilty about me being captured and Necsa's death. Is that the truth? Is it why you've been avoiding me?"

Mordred looked away. He didn't answer Amyas's question, but the way he wasn't looking at him was enough of an answer.

Amyas sighed. "None of this is your fault, and I don't blame you for any of it."

"I should have been more careful," Mordred protested. "I should have seen what Necsa was planning when we went to help the tribe. I shouldn't have left you alone."

"But you did, and you know why?"

"Because I was an idiot."

Amyas shook his head. "No. You left me alone because I asked you to. I told you to focus on the fight and that I would be fine. *I* didn't even realize what my parents and Necsa were planning. How could you have? You don't know them. I thought I did, but obviously, I was wrong. But you only did what I asked you to do, and I'm grateful for that, even with the way it ended. You did something no one ever did, which is allowing me to make my own mistakes. It wasn't nice, but I'm back home, and I'm fine."

"What about Necsa's death?"

Amyas bit his lower lip. He didn't like to think about it, even though he didn't feel guilty. "It's not going to be easy for the tribe to find another leader. Normally, Necsa's children would take her place, but she didn't have any. Necsa was a good leader, but she was terrified of looking weak, and she thought that me leaving would make that happen. I think that's why she came after me and why she tried to kill me. She could have avoided dying if she'd just let me do what I wanted, but instead, she got herself killed. I'm not angry at Thor for killing her, and I don't see why I should be angry at you."

Amyas stepped closer. He had to swallow a few times before he could continue, but when he did, he looked Mordred straight in the eyes as best as he could, considering how much taller Mordred was and the fact that he was still avoiding looking at him.

"I know you feel guilty, and that nothing I can say will make that stop. Feelings don't act that way. But it's fine. I know that in time, you'll realize that I truly am *not* angry at you and that I don't consider you responsible. I don't want to lose what's between us in the meantime. I need you right now. I lost my parents and my tribe, everything I knew before I arrived here. Right now, you're the only thing I'm sure of, and even if you have doubts, I need you to stand strong next to me if you want what we have to continue. And if you don't, just tell me."

Amyas prayed Mordred wouldn't. He didn't know how he would deal with losing Mordred, too. He supposed he would find out if it happened, but he hoped it didn't.

Mordred just stared at him, and Amyas decided to leave. He'd said what he needed to say, and now, Mordred was the one who had to take the next step.

"I love you," Amyas reminded him. "I think I'll always love you. I don't want to lose you, but if you don't feel like you can be with me anymore, that's okay. We'll go from there and deal with it."

Amyas turned toward the door. His heart felt heavy, and he was convinced that Mordred was going to tell him to leave the house. The thought was terrifying, and it was almost enough to bring Amyas to his knees.

"Wait," Mordred said.

Amyas stopped moving. He didn't turn around to look at Mordred, but like Mordred had asked, he waited. Whatever Mordred was about to say could make or break Amyas, and Amyas hoped things would go the way he needed them to.

Mordred was a selfish asshole. He should have talked to Amyas like Thor had suggested yesterday instead of sneaking out of the bedroom this morning. Last night, neither of them had been ready to talk, but Mordred shouldn't have waited until Amyas was freaked out enough to do what he'd just done.

Amyas had effectively kicked Mordred's ass. Mordred was in awe of his strength, even though Amyas shouldn't have needed it in this situation. Mordred didn't know if Amyas would ever be able to forgive him for what he'd done, but he was ready to grovel until it happened.

What had he been thinking? He suspected the answer to that was that he hadn't been. He'd only thought of himself, of how he would feel if Amyas rejected him, and he hadn't thought of how *Amyas* would feel.

He swallowed. Apologies were always hard, but he owed Amyas more than one. "I'm sorry," he said to Amyas's back. Amyas still wasn't looking at him, so Mordred had no idea what his expression was like or what he was thinking. He looked tense, though, which didn't bode well. Whatever he said or did, though, Mordred would deserve it.

Amyas finally turned around. "What are you sorry for?" he asked.

His expression was guarded, which made Mordred feel even guiltier. Amyas shouldn't feel like this, not with him. "For pushing you away. For avoiding you and not being there this morning when you woke up. For freaking out and putting distance between us. I shouldn't have."

Amyas nodded curtly. "You're right. You shouldn't have. Why did you do it, then?"

Amyas was staring, and Mordred had to resist the urge to look away. "Because I was afraid."

Amyas blinked. "What were you afraid of?"

"That you would blame me for what happened. You were under my watch, yet you were kidnapped, taken prisoner, and your tribe leader was killed."

"We already talked about that. I don't blame you for any of that. If anything, I should blame myself. I should have been more careful. I knew Necsa, and I could have guessed she would do something like this."

"But you trusted her."

"I did. But I've always known she was proud. Not being able to control me exposed her weakness, or at least, that was what she thought. It's why she came after me and why she tried to kill me. I feel guilty, but I know it wasn't my fault, and I hope that eventually, I'll get over it."

Mordred reached for Amyas. He was terrified that Amyas would move away, wouldn't want him to touch him, but thankfully, he didn't. He allowed Mordred to take his hand, and that was all Mordred dared to do right now. "What about your parents?" he asked.

Amyas shook his head. "What they did wasn't your fault, either. I trusted them, even though we never saw life the same way. I couldn't imagine they would go along with what Necsa did, but they did, and I can never trust them again. I don't even want to see them right now. Maybe in time I'll be able to forgive them, but for now, I'm not planning on going back anytime soon."

"Even though they're your family?"

"They should have thought about that before they kept me

prisoner and tried to control me. What they did wasn't out of love. They wanted to control me, and when they couldn't, they imprisoned me. How can I ever forgive that?"

"You're immortal, and so are they. You have a lot of time to forgive them."

"And maybe eventually, I will. But for now, I'm not going anywhere near them or the lake."

"Won't you miss them?" That was one more thing that scared Mordred. Amyas seemed to love the house, but there wasn't a body of water for him to spend time in. The fountain he always put his feet in wasn't enough, and while Mordred wanted to dig a pool or pond for him, he wasn't sure it would be welcome. It was still something they needed to talk about. They couldn't ignore that Amyas was an undine and used to living in a lake.

"I'll miss the lake. It was my home, and it's strange not to live there anymore. Undines are made to live both in the water and on earth, though. We wouldn't be able to marry humans otherwise. I'll be fine, even without the lake."

"And without your parents?"

Amyas rolled his eyes, which Mordred hoped meant he'd forgiven him. "I'll miss them, too," Amyas admitted. "Or maybe I'll miss the idea of them and of what we could have been as a family. Are you done? Or is there something else you're worried about?"

Mordred felt ridiculous now that everything was on the table. Amyas was right—he'd been an idiot. He shouldn't have been worried, or rather, he should have talked to Amyas about it. Amyas would have vanished Mordred's fears, and they wouldn't be doing this right now.

Maybe they'd actually needed to do it, though. They'd fallen in love, but they'd only known each other for a short amount of time. They needed to talk, and they needed to do it often. "I'll dig you a lake on the property," Mordred promised.

Amyas chuckled and moved closer, pressing his chest against Mordred's. He let go of Mordred's hands and hooked his arms around Mordred's neck, but he was short, so Mordred had to help him by cupping his ass and hauling him up. It was either that or folding himself in half, which was *not* comfortable.

Mordred turned around and put Amyas down on top of his desk. He didn't care about the files or the computer, or anything that was on it. He just wanted Amyas to be comfortable.

"I know I was an idiot," he said.

"As long as you're aware of it," Amyas answered, humor in his voice.

"I was an idiot, but I love you, and I want you in my life," Mordred continued. "You have to know it's dangerous, though. You were at the meeting, so you know everything. The conclave wants to kill me, and they won't hesitate if they get their hands on me."

"Don't you think I'm aware of that? I know the conclave is dangerous and that you're their enemy. It's one of the reasons I love you. You're convinced of what you're doing, and you're ready to die for it. I can't say it doesn't terrify me, but I can deal with it. I have to if I want to be with you, and I do. If you being an idiot isn't enough to push me away, the conclave won't be, either."

Mordred laughed and kissed Amyas. He'd almost lost him, and it would have been all his fault. He'd promised Amyas he wouldn't be an idiot again, and he would keep that promise as best as he could.

Amyas was right. If he could put up with Mordred, he would be able to put up with the conclave, too. The conclave would never stop hunting Mordred, even if Mordred decided to stop working against them. It was something everyone in his life had to learn to deal with, and apparently, it didn't scare Amyas, not beyond what was normal. It wasn't enough to push him away, something for which Mordred was grateful.

Together, they were stronger, maybe even strong enough to defeat the conclave. It wasn't going to be easy, but then, nothing worth having ever had been.

Except for Amyas. What he and Mordred had felt like the easiest thing in the world, and even though Mordred suspected that sooner or later, it would change, it made them human. They would deal with it when it happened, and if it did, they would talk things out and make up.

Mordred loved Amyas, and Amyas loved him back. Mordred was never giving that up, no matter what happened.

CHAPTER SIXTEEN

M ordred was nervous. He was used to going against the conclave, but he usually did so in the darkness. The conclave knew what he looked like, and so did his heroes, but the conclave heroes didn't. They might have seen a picture, but Mordred was different now, and he'd always liked operating in the shadows more than putting his face on display.

There was no avoiding that for the video message, though. It wasn't even a video message anymore. It was a livestream, something on which Isaac and Amyas had insisted, even though Mordred didn't understand what the difference was. The conclave wouldn't care if he was talking to them live or on a recording.

But Isaac and Amyas had insisted, and Mordred couldn't say no to Amyas, not without a good reason. He also couldn't say no to Isaac, who'd made himself right at home with the heroes. Tryg was still pouting around, glaring at anyone who came close to him, but he and Isaac were staying. So were Thor and Cecil. That made five supernatural beings living in the house now, something for which Mordred was grateful.

A few heroes were still wary, but all of them liked Isaac. He was adorable, but he was also strong. Mordred didn't know his back story, but he knew enough to be aware of the fact that it had been hell. Tryg had saved him, and just like Mordred and everyone else, he couldn't say no to the man he loved. That meant he and Isaac and all the others were staying. It felt like a new chapter in the organization Mordred had created, and he hoped it would bode well for the future.

Everything would depend on what would happen once the conclave heroes saw the stream.

"Ready?" Dimitri asked.

Mordred scowled at him, but Dimitri didn't seem to care. "Remind me why I have to do this again?" Mordred asked.

Dimitri shrugged. "Because you have a soft heart, and you couldn't say no to Amyas *and* Isaac. One of them, maybe. Both, there wasn't a chance."

Mordred huffed. "Right."

"You do realize that Amyas went to Isaac for this exact reason, right? This was his idea, but he suspected you'd be able to say no to him if he came to you on his own."

Mordred wouldn't have. "I just don't understand what difference it would have made if I'd recorded this."

Dimitri raised his hands. "Don't ask me. I'm just here for moral support."

And Mordred was grateful for it. Dimitri was Amyas's closest friend, and Mordred liked him. Mordred had kept himself apart from the heroes for a long time, except for Bayard and Eudocia, and it was strange to open himself up to other people. He wouldn't go back to how he'd been before, though. Having Amyas in his life had shown him how lonely he'd been, and he never wanted that to happen again. It wouldn't, not if he played his cards right. He was lucky Amyas had forgiven him for being an idiot, and he'd promised himself he would never do anything that would put their relationship into jeopardy again.

"If you're ready, we should start," Alger said. He was behind the camera, fiddling with it.

"I don't think I'll ever be more ready, so sure. Let's start," Mordred told him.

Alger turned his attention to Mordred. "You know how it's going to work. The camera is already on. Once we start, I'll open the stream, and this video will land on every conclave heroes' phone. They won't be able to dismiss it or trace it, although you have to make sure not to talk for too long. You have your notes?"

Mordred glared but raised his notepad. When Alger had told him that he would have only a certain amount of time to do this, he'd realized he needed to make notes. They were bullet points, and he hoped it would be enough for him to sound coherent and not like a bumbling idiot.

Alger nodded. "Good. The stream will come with an email address. The heroes will be invited to write to that address to ask for support or their questions. Hopefully, we'll get a lot of them, but I don't make any promises. That will depend on you and how convincing you are."

Mordred hoped he would be able to convince as many heroes as possible. The heroes were what made the conclave strong, and if he could take enough of them away, the conclave would be left with no manpower. They wouldn't be able to attack Mordred and his heroes or supernatural beings. They would be stuck and powerless, which was Mordred's primary goal.

"Ready?" Dimitri asked again.

Mordred's focus drifted to Amyas, who was standing against the wall, watching him. He smiled, and Mordred knew he would be ready for anything that happened in the future as long as Amyas was with him.

He looked straight at the camera. "Ready," he confirmed.

Alger raised three fingers. He counted down, lowering them one by one, then pointed straight at Mordred to tell him he was live.

Mordred swallowed. "My name is Mordred. Like all of you, I'm a hero, and I once worked for the conclave. I can imagine what they told you about me. To the conclave, I'm a traitor. I want all of you to know why I left the conclave, though, and why I'm actively working against them and against you. The conclave is lying to you."

This was easier than Mordred had expected. He barely even had to look at his notes.

"In all the legends and stories we are taught when we first arrive at the conclave, it says that heroes are created to protect the innocents, no matter who those innocents are. It can be human beings, but also supernatural beings. Not all of them are dangerous. Not all of them deserve to die, yet that's what the conclave has been doing. They kill innocent mothers, children, males who only want to protect their families. The conclave doesn't care as long as they can kill all the supernatural beings and keep their power. I know it's hard to wrap your mind around, especially when you're told, like me, that what you're doing is right. Think about it, though. Have you ever hesitated? Have you ever wondered if you were doing the right thing? If you have, you're one step closer to understanding how wrong the conclave is."

Mordred went on, explaining what had happened when he'd decided to leave and what he'd done since then. The conclave would have no doubt warned the heroes about him, but they wouldn't have explained what he was doing. They would deny it, but Mordred had proof. Alger would make sure to send everything to any hero who asked for it, and Mordred made sure to mention that as he continued talking.

"My time is almost over. I don't want the conclave to find me or the heroes who work with me. There's an email address in this message. The conclave has no way to trace it, so it's safe for you to email and ask for more details or for help. If you do, we'll make sure the conclave can't get to you. You don't have to work with me. You can decide to leave this life and stop working as a hero. No one but the conclave expects anything from you. You should be free to decide, just like everyone else. If you want to help us in our mission against the conclave, though, you'll be welcome. We're more than just heroes who work together. We're a family, and you can become part of it."

Mordred looked at Alger, nodding, and Alger nodded back. After a few seconds, he said, "It's done."

Mordred relaxed against the back of his chair. Amyas was by his side right away, cupping his face with both his hands and kissing him deeply. "I'm proud of you," he murmured.

Mordred was proud of himself, too. He should have thought about doing something like this a long time ago, but as long as he'd done it, who had thought about it, and when, didn't matter.

"Emails are starting to come in," Alger said. "It's going to take a while to answer all of them, and I don't think I'll be able to do that on my own."

"Recruit anyone you want. This is important, and I want us to answer every single email. The heroes out there asking questions are the ones we need to help and reach out to." And hopefully, now that they knew what the conclave was doing, they would leave the conclave behind and do the right thing. For those who didn't, though, Mordred wouldn't hesitate. If he ever had to fight any of them, he would make sure he won.

He had too much to come back to. He'd gotten Amyas back after almost losing him, and he wasn't giving him or anything in his life up, not to the conclave.

Never again.

You may also enjoy the following from eXtasy Books Inc:

Water, Air and Fire
Catherine Lievens

Excerpt

Matias held his breath. There was nothing else he could do, not if he didn't want to be found. He hadn't meant to spy on his mother and her boss, yet here he was, holding a sandwich and having to listen to what they were saying so they wouldn't notice him.

"You already know they're part of it," Matias's mother said.

"They're my grandsons."

"You never cared about them. Why start now? They can ruin everything, and I don't want that to happen."

There was a pause, then Mr. Long said, "I'm the one making decisions here."

Matias could almost see his mother press her lips together. She no doubt had a lot to say, but she wouldn't. She wouldn't put her job in jeopardy. "Of course," she agreed. "You're the head of Purity. I would never dream of trying to step in. I just want to be sure you're not acting too softly since they're your grandsons."

Matias bit his lower lip. There had been hints of his mother and Mr. Long working with Purity earlier in the conversation, but he hadn't wanted to believe it. Maybe he should have. It didn't make much sense when it came to his mother, but Mr. Long was different. He didn't like Matias, even though he'd known him since he was a kid. Matias was pretty sure that if it were for him, he'd kick him out and never think about him again.

"Who they are doesn't matter," Mr. Long snapped. "It never did. If they don't listen to me, they'll pay for it."

"They stood up to you the last time they were here."

There was a slam as if Mr. Long had hit his desk, which Matias thought could have happened. "They won't for long. I'll make sure they pay for that. How can they ruin everything like this?"

"They're mixing."

Mr. Long snorted. "That's not what I'm talking about. Who cares? It's not like they're going to have children anyway."

"Because their mates are men." The disgust dripped from Matias's mother's voice.

He pressed his lips together and closed his eyes for a moment. He'd never come out to his mother, afraid of the way she would react. He'd known she wouldn't accept it, and today was confirming that. She would hate him if she found out he was gay. Maybe she hated him anyway, considering how he was born and what he could do.

"I can't allow that to be known. Can you imagine the scorn if someone were to find out?"

"I think people have already found out."

"I'll find a way to make them pay," Mr. Long promised. "The attacks against them went badly, and we lost eight men, but we have others."

"Not enough. We lost too many in the attacks on Henry and Edward."

"Then recruit more. With what we're planning, we're going to need all the manpower we can get."

"And I'll help you as much as I can. I'm in this a hundred percent."

They were silent for a moment, and Matias wondered if it was safe for him to sneak away. He was in the hallway just outside Mr. Long's office. He'd been going back to his bedroom after getting a sandwich in the kitchen, and he'd noticed the door open. He'd been planning on walking by without stopping when he'd heard what his mother and her boss were saying.

When he'd realized they were talking of Purity and Mr. Long's grandsons, he'd stopped. Once he understood how serious the conversation was, he'd known his mother would do something if she found out he had heard it.

He couldn't walk in front of the office. He could hear the sound of kissing now, and while it made his stomach churn, he knew they would be busy for a while. Still, he didn't want to risk it, so he slowly walked backward until he was sure no one in the office would be able to see him. He dropped the sandwich he was still holding onto a table that was set against the wall. He wasn't hungry anymore.

"We should take this to the other room," Matias's mother purred.

Matias grimaced, but he listened to her and Mr. Long leave the office. There was a small sitting room next to it, with a door between them, which meant they didn't have to step into the hallway.

The door slammed behind them, and Matias took a step forward. He knew it was dangerous, but he risked a peek into the office. His shoulders slumped when he saw it was empty. Then, he heard a giggle coming from the sitting room, followed by a moan. They were going to be busy for a while, yet Matias hesitated.

If he did what he was planning, he wouldn't be able to stay. He would lose the one place he'd been able to call home since he was a child. He couldn't stand by and do nothing, though.

He rushed toward the desk. He had no idea what he was

doing, but at least he was doing something. He sat behind the desk, lost for a second before he gathered his thoughts. He opened the first drawer, snatched a USB key from it, and pushed it into the computer. Luckily for him, Mr. Long often had problems with the computer, and he always asked Matias to take care of it. Matias had never snooped, but maybe he should have.

He started now, clicking around on the computer, copying everything he could to the key while looking at the documents on the desk. He doubted Mr. Long had anything important in plain sight, but he still grabbed a few things. He needed to get out of here now. The moaning was becoming louder, and he knew his mother and her boss were going to be done soon.

He finished copying what he could, snatched the key out of the computer, grabbed the documents, and left. His heart raced, but of course, this was where his luck ended. He heard the door open behind him, then his mother called out, "Matias?"

Matias ignored her and ran.

He and his mother had rooms in the wing of the house reserved to the help. They weren't the only ones who lived there. Mr. Long's cooks, his gardeners, and everyone else did, too. Thankfully for Matias, no one noticed him rushing in, and he managed to get to his room and close the door without a problem.

He leaned against the door. He didn't know what to do, or rather, he knew what to do, but he didn't want to do it. It felt like a betrayal, and he had no idea how he would deal with everything once he did, but he also couldn't just stand by and do nothing. Edward and Henry were in trouble, and it was the kind of trouble that could mean death for them. Matias wasn't going to allow that to happen.

He, Edward, and Henry weren't friends, but they were friendly. It wasn't only that, though. Matias had always disliked what Purity was doing. He was the fruit of a relationship between two people who wielded different elements, and Purity thought he shouldn't exist.

His mother and Mr. Long thought he shouldn't exist.

Matias realized he was still holding the USB key and the documents, and he put everything on the dresser. Then, he took his cell phone out. He knew what he had to do, even though he was terrified.

He unlocked his phone and found the number he was looking for. His hand trembled as he raised the phone to his ear, and he did his best to listen to make sure no one was coming his way. Mr. Long never came to their rooms, but Matias's mother had seen him, and she'd want an explanation.

"Hello?" Henry said.

Matias swallowed, but it didn't help his dry mouth. "Henry? You told me I could call you if I needed you." And Matias definitely needed him right now.

"Matias. I expect you to call sooner."

Matias chuckled darkly. He probably should have.

"I'm glad you called, though," Henry continued. "What can I do for you?"

"I need help. I'm on the run." Because Matias needed to leave. There was no way he could stay, not when Mr. Long and his mother would probably get rid of him if they found out he knew about Purity.

"Tell me what's going on."

Matias was relieved Henry believed him. He wanted to know what was going on, which was only natural, but he didn't doubt Matias's word. "I didn't mean to find this out. I heard the conversation," he explained.

"A conversation?" a second voice said.

Matias frowned. "Edward?" He asked because he was pretty sure this was Henry's brother. He hadn't realized Henry had put the phone on speaker, but he supposed it made sense.

"I put the phone on speaker," Henry explained. "Tell us what happened. Tell us what we can do to help."

Matias swallowed again. "My mother. She was talking with Melchior." He almost said Mr. Long, but he was already talking to two of them, and they would understand better if he called their grandfather by his given name. "They're the heads of Purity, Henry." The words stumbled out. Matias should probably have found a better way to tell Henry and Edward that their grandfather was a monster, but he couldn't keep his secret to himself one more second.

"What do you know what Purity?" Henry asked.

"Not much. They were talking about it, though, and I know it was important. They were angry because the attack against you went badly. They lost another eight people, and they don't have a lot of people to begin with. They're planning something." Matias hesitated. He needed to tell someone about this, and Henry and Edward were probably the best people. "I waited until they were gone, that I went into the office. I grabbed all the documents I could find. I even managed to copy part of the stuff that's on Melchior's computer."

"Why would you do that? It's dangerous," Henry protested.

"Because they attacked you. I knew what I was doing. Only they found out, and I had to run. I need help." His mother might try to talk to him on her own first, but Matias knew how Mr. Long would react if she told him what she'd seen. This place wasn't safe for Matias anymore.

"And you have it," Henry said. "Don't worry about it. We'll take care of you. Just tell us where you are, and we'll find you."

Matias relaxed. Henry was going to help him, and he would be able to get away from his house.

"Where are you?" Henry asked.

"Still at home, but I'm leaving." And he was never coming back.

About the Author

Catherine is the creator of several series, most of them paranormal, including the Whitedell Pride Series and the Gillham Pack Series. While she graduated in translation, she decided to go the writer's way because it was more fun to create her own stories and characters.

She's been living in Italy for more than twenty years, but she's a daughter of the North—Belgium to be precise—and she misses it so much that she's already planning to move back.

She loves pizza—probably too much—her son, her pets, and of course, books. She sneaks some reading time into her schedule every time she has five minutes free from writing, demands from her various pets and son, and lastly, housework.

Connect with her:

lievens.catherine@gmail.com
BookBub: https://www.bookbub.com/authors/catherine-lievens
Website: https://authorcatherinelievens.com/
Facebook: https://www.facebook.com/catherine.lievens.9
Facebook Group: https://www.facebook.com/groups/411788002341528/
Twitter: https://twitter.com/authorCLievens
Newsletter: https://authorcatherinelievens.com/newsletter/